$20.00

Thieves Never Steal in the Rain

D1075996

Essential Prose Series 120

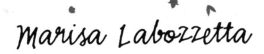

Thieves Never Steal in the Rain

Marisa Labozzetta

GUERNICA
EDITIONS
TORONTO • BUFFALO • LANCASTER (U.K.)
2016

LONGWOOD PUBLIC LIBRARY

Copyright © 2016, Marisa Labozzetta and Guernica Editions Inc.
All rights reserved. The use of any part of this publication,
reproduced, transmitted in any form or by any means, electronic,
mechanical, photocopying, recording or otherwise stored in a
retrieval system, without the prior consent of the publisher is an
infringement of the copyright law.

Michael Mirolla, editor
Cover and interior design, David Moratto
Guernica Editions Inc.
1569 Heritage Way, Oakville, (ON), Canada L6M 2Z7
2250 Military Road, Tonawanda, N.Y. 14150-6000 U.S.A.
www.guernicaeditions.com

Distributors:
University of Toronto Press Distribution,
5201 Dufferin Street, Toronto (ON), Canada M3H 5T8
Gazelle Book Services, White Cross Mills, High Town,
Lancaster LA1 4XS U.K.

First edition.
Printed in Canada.

Legal Deposit—First Quarter
Library of Congress Catalog Card Number: 2015949358
Library and Archives Canada Cataloguing in Publication
Labozzetta, Marisa, author
Thieves never steal in the rain / Marisa Labozzetta.
—First edition.

(Essential prose series ; 120)
Short stories.
ISBN 978-1-77183-050-8 (paperback)

I. Title. II. Series: Essential prose series ; 120

PS3562.A2356T45 2016   813'.54   C2015-905884-8

For Ethan and Luke

Contents

Villa Foresta

I t was raining on the Good Friday they arrived in Rome, coming down with a vengeance. The agent at the car rental said it had been going on like that for three days: water pooling in the narrow streets as well as in the piazzas; low temperatures and wind—unseasonable weather for March.

They had already dived head first into a disagreement about whether to purchase car insurance. Elliott hated paying the exorbitant fee; he liked to gamble that way. Of course, there was the time someone hit their passenger door at an Auto Grill in Naples while they were inside buying prosciutto and provolone panini. Two days later, someone stole the side-view mirror at a remote *agriturismo*. The damages had cost twice as much as the week's rental fee.

"But that was in the south," Elliott said. "What's the chance of it happening here?"

"Sure. No one ever has accidents in central Italy," Joanna said. "And everyone is honest."

It irked him the way she played by the rules. She paid her bills the day they arrived. Elliot, on the other hand, wrote the due dates of his on their envelopes, which he kept in chronological order on his desk and mailed no more than three days in advance. Occasionally he forgot and had to pay a late fee. It infuriated her, but Elliott shrugged off the loss as a fair exchange for the interest he usually earned from money that remained in his bank account rather than in that of some utility or credit card company. He took the insurance this time, however; anything to make her happy these days.

She pulled the lapels of her raincoat tighter as they drove on the *autostrada*, unable to rid herself of the clamminess and feeling like a damsel in a British movie in need of the only cure for such ills—a cup of tea. He turned on the heat with some reluctance. After all, it was spring.

A fuzzy handwritten fax with directions to the villa lay on her lap. They were expected for dinner that evening; with a good hour-and-forty-minute drive ahead of them, she fished in her bag for some trail mix.

The travel bag had too many compartments, and it took her forever to locate anything, from her passport to a pack of gum. After unzipping and zipping several pockets, she handed Elliott an open sandwich bag from which he took a fistful of the contents, nearly emptying it. She, for her part, put a single almond or raisin into her mouth and rolled it around until she extracted all the saltiness or sweetness it had to offer. She then bit into its new softer state and chewed it well before swallowing. Each colorful M&M lay on her tongue like the Eucharistic host and remained there until the outer coating dissolved, leaving only the smooth chocolate center. The dry bump of chocolate clung to her tongue, grew smaller and smaller, and, when she could hold on to it no longer, vanished. As the commercial used to say: "Melts in your mouth, not in your hand."

Of course they never melted in Elliott's hand, since he shoveled a mound of Trail Mix into his mouth, and with a few loud chews and a giant swallow, it was gone, sucked in like dirt up a vacuum cleaner hose. Although he denied it, she knew that eating was how he dealt with Jill's death. He had gained 35 pounds since the accident; he weighed 220 and counting.

He took another handful of trail mix and caught her look of disapproval. "What?" He barked.

She didn't answer.

"I eat too much. I'm a pig. That's what you think, isn't it? That's what you've always thought."

"It's not healthy."

"Nuts? Raisins?"

"Elliott."

"I know, Joanna. Everything in moderation. That's your motto. Better yet, that's your father's motto—the Marco Ficola motto."

"You know what I think."

"It's sublimation. So what if it is? You, on the other hand, can't let go of anything."

"That's right. Make light of your vice even if it ends up killing you."

"I've got to make light of something. You carry enough pessimism around to sink both of us."

His last sentence rang out loud and clear, uttered in the cessation of the rain as they entered a long mountain tunnel. She became claustrophobic in tunnels, and Elliott always tried to talk her through them. Even now, he made the effort.

"The Italians might have known that you can't move mountains, but they sure figured out how to barrel through them," he said. Once, in the Brooklyn Battery Tunnel, he'd actually managed to make her laugh.

***

It had long grown dark by the time they exited the *autostrada*. They sat for a few moments at a confluence of several smaller roads, studying a totem pole of signs that pointed in various directions. The "Gronda" sign seemed to suggest a road to the left. Elliott turned. After a while they came to a dead end and a decaying factory. Elliott drove back to the intersection. His stomach growled; a hunger headache throbbed at Joanna's temples. They took another wrong road and returned to the intersection. No one from whom they might ask directions appeared.

Elliott had insisted on booking a room at Villa Foresta, but Joanna would have been content to stay with her family. How could she pass up the chance to be alone with him in a bed in a hotel room? He had asked. How was it any different than being alone in their own bed in their own house? She wanted to know. Did hotel rooms do weird things to all men? Signal torrid lovemaking, hedonism unattainable in daily living? That was unfair: there was a time when she too had relished the chance to hole up with Elliott for several days, but that seemed like a lifetime ago. Before marriage. Before the birth of their daughter. Before her death. Now Joanna just took each day as it came—her breath held in anticipation, as though the future were perched high on a cliff, ready at the least provocation to sail down, crash into the ocean, and be silenced forever. She wondered how two people who had loved so passionately could have such misconceptions about each other, how a common grief could push them apart.

"We should have stayed at my aunt and uncle's. You know they won't hide the fact that we've insulted them," she said.

"It's an act."

"I can't believe you said that."

"It's true. Your father told me."

"Well, I can't believe he said that about his own brother. He just gets upset that this brother never visits the brothers who live in the States."

"He's got a point. Yet you and your father keep coming here."

"We love it here."

Up hills, down hills, around bends, through a small town, into desolation. The fog was thick and eerie. Why did they always end up searching for a place to stay in pitch blackness? Everything was so much more difficult in the dark, laden with a sense of urgency and desperation.

"Let's return to Go and start over," she said.

"Just a little longer." Elliott dragged out the words as though he were talking to a patient he was stitching up in the ER.

After about a mile, a sign on their left indicated the villa. The gate was open, smoke rose from the chimney. They drove up the graveled drive to the long stone building and parked beside a horseshoe-shaped wooden portal.

Thanks to a lengthy layover in Zurich, they had been traveling for nearly 26 hours, and she just wanted to stop moving. Lately, a growing antsiness afflicted her on trips; being confined for longer than two hours nearly drove her crazy. Elliott loved long car rides; he loved to travel. So had she once, but she'd become restless, fidgeting in her seat like a toddler. At least on planes she could read, or use the excuse of avoiding jet lag to drug herself. In cars, however, it was impossible to glance at print without being over-whelmed by nausea, and beyond the first hour Elliott and Joanna fell silent.

***

"*Buonasera!*" Joanna called out, her voice bouncing around the terra-cotta floors, the white plaster walls, the dark wooden beams. She inhaled the aroma of roasting meat.

"*Buonasera*," someone sang from the kitchen beyond the vacant dining room.

In a moment, Paolo appeared, rubbing his hands together in eagerness to greet his guests, then pushing his black-rimmed glasses further up the bridge of his nose to see his guests more clearly. "Signora Ficola, *benvenuta*."

"This is my husband, Elliott," she said in Italian.

"*Benvenuto*, Signor Ficola."

Elliott stammered in the little Italian he knew to ex-plain that his surname was not Ficola but Blake. He failed and remained Signor Ficola.

Paolo didn't ask for their passports or give them iden-tification cards to fill out. She couldn't tell if he was acting out of kindness, since they stood before him like two refu-gees emerging from a tempest, or negligence.

He pointed to their bags. "Leave everything here for now. Come. I've prepared a special dinner for you. *Prego*."

They followed him into the dining room, where a table set for two faced a large hearth in which a few flames struggled with damp wood. Still, the fire cast off enough heat to warm them. When she told Paolo that it smelled good, he smiled with pride, the eyes behind his glasses widening.

"Are there any other guests?" she asked.

"Only you. It's still off-season." His gaze lingered on them for an awkward moment as though he were waiting for them to ask another question. Then he returned to the kitchen.

"Odd fella," Elliott said. "Did you notice his hands? They're enormous for such a little guy. He looks like Mickey Mouse."

"You know what they say about big hands."

"I'd like to disprove that theory once and for all," Elliott said, an allusion to his small hands and ample penis.

The demanding weight of expectation rose around them like the fog they had just escaped. No other guests to wonder about, whose relationships they could conjecture upon, and on whose childrearing capabilities they could pass judgment. No conversations on which to eavesdrop. No other lives to imagine. Just Elliott and Joanna.

***

Paolo brought their antipasto: a plate filled with crostini, hot peppers stuffed with tuna and a slice of prosciutto.

"Do you like *pappardelle*?"

"Oh yes," she said.

"I've prepared it especially for you. But I confess that the peppers are sent from my mother."

The pasta, light and topped with a smattering of tomato sauce, slid down their throats.

She had been starving, and she ate so fast that, by the time the grilled sausages came, she could barely finish one. She gave the remaining two to Elliott, who downed them along with his own three, the potatoes, and green salad.

"Now I have a very special dessert for you." Paolo added that it too had been made by his mother. He brought them fruit fermented in liquor, and some biscotti.

While the meal was delicious, it was simpler than Joanna had expected to be served at an inn. It was as though Paolo had tried to make as elegant a meal as he could from staples and his mother's leftovers.

After dinner, Elliott went back to the car for the luggage. Since they were the only guests and it was raining, Paolo said they could leave the car out front for the night instead of in the parking lot down the hill.

"Did you lock the car door?" Joanna asked Elliott when he returned dripping wet once again.

"Don't worry, signora," Paolo said. "Thieves never steal in the rain. If they were that ambitious, they would get a real job."

Elliott smiled when she translated; she knew he was thinking that perhaps he and Paolo were of like minds. Elliott carried the bags upstairs.

Joanna moved her chair directly in front of the fireplace, kicked off her shoes, and placed her feet on the low wall of the hearth. She began to peel the chestnuts Paolo had roasted in the fire. Chestnuts. They were something her father prepared every holiday. He used a sharp paring knife and made a cross through the shell. Then he soaked the chestnuts in water and waited until the family was just about to sit at the table before he put them into the oven.

Sometimes he forgot them and they burned; sometimes he forgot to put them into the oven altogether. But there were times when they were warm and soft and smooth, and the shell slipped right off when you peeled it back from the starlike points of the cross that had curled upward.

She thought of her father now, back in Boston recovering from pneumonia. He was too weak to make the trip to be with his youngest brother, who had remained in Italy with Joanna's grandparents when her father and the rest of his brothers emigrated. She'd had trouble deciding whether or not she should be away from her father at this time, which was probably why she had come: to lighten the onus of responsibility and, of course, to satisfy Elliott's desire for them to get away. Her mother was with her father; they hadn't left each other's side for as long as Joanna could remember—just in case. If something were to happen to him in her mother's absence, after fifty-two years of marriage, she would never have been able to forgive herself. Growing up, Joanna had thought their relationship smothering. They were co-dependents in neuroses, always waiting for the other shoe to drop in a fatalistic approach to life Joanna could never, as a young adult, comprehend. Now she coveted the endearment in their fear of letting go.

Joanna hadn't been with Jill when she died, and in the last three and a half years barely a night had gone by without her dreaming about her daughter. Parents are supposed to protect their offspring, ward off evil spirits. If you turn away from the crib for a second, she might suffocate. If you send her up on that jungle gym and blink, you might miss her fall.

Joanna's father, however, hadn't tried to stop Joanna from attending his brother's anniversary party, though she knew he worried whenever she went away. Before she left, he would dig his calloused hands into her shoulders and stare into her eyes as though he might never see them again: something might happen to him and she wouldn't be there; something might happen to her.

"Is there anything else I can get for you?" Paolo asked.

"I'm never moving from this spot," she told him.

"You like the fire?" He was pleased.

"Very much."

"*Che tempaccio!*" He indicated the beating of the rain against the windows.

"What's the forecast?"

"Three more days of the same."

"What time is breakfast?" she asked.

"Whenever you like, signora." He waved his hands in the air as if to say: What does it matter? You're the only ones here.

"Eight-thirty or nine?"

"*Va bene.*"

They said goodnight. She tore herself away from the fire and went up to the apartment and Elliott.

***

With their pick of apartments in the empty villa, and all for the same price, they had chosen the largest of the three. It was ridiculously big for two people: two living rooms of substantial size, a bedroom, a full kitchen, and a big sun-room with a dining set. Elliott was already asleep, fully clothed on the bed, when she arrived. He had placed her suitcase on a chair and unzipped it for her. She fumbled through it in the dark, feeling for the silk of her pajamas, and undressed in the bathroom so as not to wake him. She was too tired to wash. In her head she heard a movie star she had once seen on TV explain the secret of her flawless complexion: "Never, never, no matter how tired I am or how late it is, do I go to bed without washing my face."

"Well, lady, you're a better woman than I am—or a liar," Joanna whispered.

In bed, she studied her husband as her eyes adjusted to the dark: sparse strands of hair, translucent eyelids, wafer-thin cheeks veined with fine red capillaries. Everything appeared so delicate, everything but his belly, which seemed to be growing like a woman's whose gestation was the time that had elapsed since Jill's death. By Joanna's calculations, he would have been forty-two months pregnant. She tried to remember the excitement she'd felt during their first years together, when her attraction to this slender, calm, and very American-looking man had nearly consumed her. It should have been just an affair, she decided.

They lay there, the bed linens a barrier between them. He slipped his hand under the sheet and it found its way to one of her breasts.

"You should get undressed," she said.

"So should you," he mumbled, eyes still closed.

"I am."

"Mmm." The cadence of this murmur indicated disappointment that she was wearing anything at all.

"Someday I'd like you to come to bed naked."

"You know I need to warm up first."

"After all that time in front of the fire, I'd say you ought to be well done."

"It's late for us," she whispered, meaning the time change. "Too late?"

Even in his semiconscious state he knew the weight of that question. She didn't know the answer. Worse, she didn't know if she cared to know the answer. Their relationship had lost its priority. What she hungered for—her only child—was out of reach, and, at her age, so were her chances for another. The distributor had run out of stock, the manufacturer had stopped producing. We're out of business; you'll have to do without, they said. Do without. That was something she'd heard repeatedly as a child. In the Depression, her family had done without. During the war in Italy, they'd done without. When they first came to the States, they did without. Doing without made them strong and industrious. It built character. It proved that family was all one really needed in life. But she also remembered her mother telling her, when their next-door neighbor had had an affair that sent her husband packing with the children, that a woman could live without her husband but never without her children. It had been a warning to Joanna to behave in her marriage—to watch her step, to let him be the one to stray. However, Elliott and she had been faithful to one another, yet both no longer had their child.

***

It was still drizzling the following morning. Joanna glanced at the alarm clock on the nightstand; it was five to eleven, and Elliott was gone. She showered, pulled her dark brown ringlets back into a ponytail, lined her sable eyes with a black pencil, and her covered her lips with clear gloss before she got dressed. Elliott had arranged his clothes on the shelves in the armoire. He always unpacked, even for one night; she never did. Good thing, because he used up most of the drawers. She did remove the dress she planned to wear to the anniversary party and hung that alongside his suit, draped her shawl around the dress's shoulders, and placed her fancy pumps beneath it. She's all ready to go, she thought, Joanna the invisible lady. That was what she'd become.

There was no table set in the dining room.

"*Buongiorno*, signora. I just took away everything. I thought you didn't want breakfast, but I can set it out again." Paolo startled her. She hadn't heard his footsteps on the tile floor because he was wearing sneakers. He had a navy blue running suit on. "La *ginastica*," he said, explaining that he ran every morning.

"Would you mind?" Despite stuffing herself the night before, she was famished.

"But of course. No problem. Cappuccino, espresso?"

"Cappuccino, please."

"Juice?"

"No, thank you."

As he set a basket of warmed rolls and some butter and marmalade on the table, he told her that Signor Ficola had left a message for her. He had gone for a short hike but would be back before noon to take her to Deruta.

"You understood him?" She fixated on the black hairs that seemed to be growing, as they spoke, out of his sleeves and onto the backs of those big hands.

"He made himself understood." Paolo made a swooping gesture to indicate that Elliott had pantomimed his intentions.

"Do you remember what time that was?" she asked.

"Around nine. Not a very good day for a hike. I tried myself but I gave up early on. I drove to Acquasparta instead to the butcher in case you intended to have dinner here tonight."

"The weather doesn't bother Elliott. He likes the outdoors."

"*È bravo* Signor Ficola. I like him." He spoke the last words in heavily accented English.

"Yes. He's a good man. Where did you learn to speak English?"

He laughed and reverted to Italian. "I don't. I'm trying to teach myself. I watch American movies. It's difficult to run this villa without English: mostly British and Americans come. You know we Italians don't speak many languages. Those who do prefer to work in the real-estate business than an inn." He rubbed his thumb, index, and middle fingers together the way her father did whenever he talked about money.

"Paolo, does your family own the villa?"

"No, signora. Two Neapolitans bought it several years ago from the New Zealand couple who restored it. I've watched it since I was a child, through its decadence to its renovation." He paused then said with rapture: "Villa Foresta has been my fascination. I helped build all those steps going down to the parking lot." The big hands were held out now, palms up, for display. There was anxiety in his eyes when he mentioned the steps and the former owners, and he seemed on the verge of telling her more about them, but then thought better of it.

"Do you mind if I call my family? I forgot to charge my cell."

"*Prego*, signora." Paola gestured for her to use the hall phone.

She had begun to search for the address book in her voluminous bag when her peripheral vision caught sight of something at the top of the stairs. It was a little girl sitting in the middle of the staircase, her big brown eyes fixed on Joanna's face. The child's hands worked the movable legs of the kind of painted wooden horse they sold at souvenir shops or crafts tents during the Christmas season.

"*Ciao*," Joanna said.

"*Ciao*." Bashful, the child looked down at the horse and made it gallop on her lap.

"*What's your name?*" Joanna asked.

"Elisabetta," she said, still focused on the horse.

"Elisabetta, *vieni qua!*" A woman's voice called from above.

"Is that your mother?"

The girl nodded.

"She wants you."

Elisabetta grinned before she scurried up the stairs.

"Who's the child?" she asked Paolo when she returned to the dining room. He was behind the bar, wiping the steamer nozzle of the cappuccino machine with a damp cloth.

"Elisabetta?"

"Yes."

They could hear the frustrated woman upstairs ordering her daughter to be still.

"She's always underfoot, that little girl. But she's adorable. Her mother is too young to appreciate her. A pity. The mother cleans the villa."

Joanna inclined her head, signaling her interest.

"Listen, signora, and I will tell you." He placed his forearms on the counter and leaned into them, pushing up the black eyeglasses. She took a sip of cappuccino and licked the sweet foam from her upper lip.

"There were times during its renovation when the New Zealand couple left—he on business; she back to New Zealand—and their son came to stay. That's when Villa Foresta turned into a hell filled with ugly people. Very ugly people. Filth. Needles everywhere. You can imagine what went on here. Would you like another cappuccino?"

"No, thank you. Actually I'd really like a cup of tea." The coffee was for some reason nauseating her.

"Chamomile? You don't feel well?"

"Black tea, if you have it, would be wonderful."

"Signora, this is Villa Foresta. At Villa Foresta, all things are possible!"

"The child?"

"Domenica got involved with the owner's son." Then he said in English: "He knocked her up. I say it right, no?"

"You said it right. It's just not—you said it right."

"But you play with fire, you get burned." He went back to speaking Italian. "She's a nice girl, signora. These things happen. Domenica never told the boy or his parents: she was too ashamed. They all had their own problems anyway." He looked around, as though someone might be listening, and whispered: "Crazy people. The boy's father is buried out under those stairs that go to the parking lot. His wish. Crazy people."

Joanna was about to ask how the villa's former owner had died when the front door creaked open and Elliott came into the dining room. "You should come out," he said. "It's clearing up. What a view here! We couldn't appreciate it last night. Did you bring your paints?"

"You know I didn't." She hadn't painted since Jill's death.

"We can pick some up. Or at least a sketch pad."

"Don't push, Elliott." She was glaring at him now. She would paint when she was ready.

"Will you be dining here this evening?" Paolo asked. He seemed relieved when she told him that they were going to Orvieto.

"Paolo! Paolo!" Elisabetta came running down the stairs. "Mamma says I can have a *biscotto*. Please."

"Un *biscotto*? *Mannaggia*." Paolo eyed her warily then smiled. "*Va bene. Ecco*." He handed her the cookie, for which she thanked him.

"Look at her, Elliott."

"Cute."

"No, look at her. Who does she remind you of?"

"Joanna," he said, begging.

"Really."

"A little."

"No. A lot."

"We need to get going if you want to go to Deruta and still eat in Orvieto tonight," Elliott said.

"Paolo, do you think Elisabetta could come with us —just to Deruta?" Joanna asked.

"Joanna!" Elliott cried.

"To Deruta?" Paolo asked with surprise.

"Just for a little while. Maybe the mother would like it if we got her out of her hair."

He called up to Domenica, who came down with the stairs with their used sheets and towels over her arms. She was petite, a child herself, not more than 19 or 20. She had the same reddish brown hair as Elisabetta, pulled back but with strands escaping, though her face was not as delicate as the child's and her skin was darker.

"I realize you don't know us, but we're only going out for an hour or two. I was wondering if Elisabetta could come with us."

Domenica cast a bewildered look at Paolo.

"She's a *paisana*," Paolo said. "Even Renato the butcher knows the family."

These people were like two innocents, Joanna thought: one terribly young, the other unworldly and naïve. Domenica was torn between having time to get her work done and trusting two complete strangers. But she was weary, and time meant money. Joanna would not have done it, she thought, but what good had overprotection gotten her?

Domenica consented.

"That is, if she wants to come," Joanna said.

"Do you want to go with the nice lady and her husband to Deruta?" Domenica asked, as blandly as if she had asked her daughter if she needed to go to the bathroom.

At first Elisabetta was hesitant, like a kitten leaning in and rubbing her body against her mother's side. Then, looking up at Joanna with those big eyes, she smiled as though Joanna were holding out a whole package of *biscotti* to her. Joanna took her hand.

"Does she have a jacket?" Joanna asked.

Domenica went into the kitchen and came back with a heavy blue sweater. Blue had been Jill's favorite color.

"Joanna, this is ridiculous." Elliott said.

Joanna ignored him.

"Leave this here." Domenica took the wooden horse from her daughter and put on her sweater. But once her hand had gone through the sleeve, the child picked the horse right back up.

Outside, the vista spread out before them: tones of umber left over from winter mixed with the green of rolling hills. It was miraculous. Joanna took Elisabetta's hand. "How old are you?" she asked.

Elisabetta held up three fingers. "And a half," she added.

***

Deruta was a strange town. Apart from the historic center filled with artisan shops, it was a long stretch of roadway lined with hotels and factories displaying colorful majolica: platters, vases, four-foot planters, dinnerware, oil and vinegar cruets, pitchers, clocks, and more, all intricately patterned.

"I don't really need anything," Joanna told Elliott.

"There must be something you'd like. You always get something." Elliott had been intent on coming here. Oddly enough, he liked rituals, and Deruta had been one of their pilgrimages whenever they came to visit her family.

Joanna picked up a butter dish with hand-painted orange, yellow, and blue birds on it.

"Want that?" Elliott was quick to ask.

"I don't know. What do you think, Elisabetta? Do you think I should buy this? Do you think it's pretty?"

She nodded, eyes filled with longing.

"Okay, then. We'll take it. Do you think your mother would like one too?" she asked.

The child's face brightened. "*Sì!*"

As the saleswoman secured the dishes in bubble wrap, an elderly priest entered the shop. In a slow but determined gait, the little man came directly to them, the only customers. He lifted his right hand and, making the sign of the cross in front of each one of them, blessed them in the name of the Father, Son, and Holy Spirit.

"*Buona Pasqua,*" he concluded. "*E buona giornata.*"

"Happy Easter to you too, Father," Joanna said, feeling complete for the first time in nearly four years. He had taken them for a family. He wandered out in search of others on whom to bestow his blessings.

They went to a bar and bought Elisabetta some gelato. Joanna had coffee, Elliott a glass of orange juice.

"When is your birthday?" Joanna asked Elisabetta.

"June—no, July," she quickly corrected herself.

"July what?"

"Twelve," she said proudly.

Elliott cast that disapproving look at his wife.

"What?"

"Don't even go there," he warned.

"Would you like to see a picture of my little girl?" Joanna asked Elisabetta.

"For Chrissake." Elliott turned away.

"I'm just showing her Jill's picture." She took a preschool photo, along with Jill's high school graduation picture—the last formal one taken of her, out of her wallet and held them in front of Elisabetta. "Do you think she looks like you?"

She nodded.

"What do you want her to say?" Elliott barked.

"Admit it, Elliott. She looks like Jill."

"What's your point? She's from the same region as your family. Half the women here look like you."

"What about the horse?"

"All children have rocking horses and toys like that."

He had said he would wait out her depression for as long as it took. He had even supported her meditation class with a popular clairvoyant, although he never bought the philosophy of reincarnation that she adopted, the idea that the spirit went on and on, over and over again, in different host bodies. No. He just didn't buy it. Nor did he buy the thought of an afterlife or communication with the spirit of the dead. He was a man of science, and while science had not been able to save his child, who had been thrown from the horse he had bought her, he would not resort to some spiritual crutch. He believed in doing good deeds here on earth. Anything after that was pure speculation with which he would not compromise himself.

"It is good to see you smile," he said.

After Elisabetta fell asleep in the backseat, Joanna told Elliott the story Paolo had recounted to her.

"The family doesn't even know she exists. Isn't that sad, Elliott?"

He took his eyes off the road for a second and looked at her. "Yes," he said.

At Villa Foresta, Paolo was laboring over a fax he was going to send to an American woman. He handed it to Joanna and asked if she would please translate a sentence.

"Come, Elisabetta, I'll take you home to Mamma," Paolo said. "Did you have a good day?"

The child was suddenly bubbling with commentary about the butter dish, the ice cream, and the priest, as though she had saved it all in a treasure box until now.

"If we don't see you tonight, we'll see each other tomorrow morning," Paolo said. "You leave the following day?"

"Yes. Monday morning," Joanna confirmed.

"*Peccato.*" Too bad.

She crouched down and took Elisabetta into her arms and kissed her on both cheeks. Joanna made a point of not saying goodbye.

"Will she and Domenica be here tomorrow morning?" she asked.

"No, signora. Tomorrow is Easter Sunday."

"Of course. I forgot. How stupid of me. What about Monday?"

"Certo! After the holiday, every morning, signora. Guests or no guests—there's always work at Villa Foresta."

***

She rose before Elliott did on Easter Sunday, happy for the first time in a very long while, excited to get out of bed, a heaviness no longer hanging in the air. Instead of going down to the dining room, she took advantage of the apartment amenities. There was a jar of instant coffee on the counter; she put a spoonful into a cup and scalded a little of the milk they had bought the day before. Trying not to wake Elliott, she quietly rummaged through the cupboards. She wanted Elliott to rest, but she also wanted time to explore her new surroundings. Where were the pots? How did the burners ignite? She had always enjoyed this challenge when they vacationed—Mama Bear foraging on a mountainside for her family's survival.

She wished that it were Monday, because she couldn't wait to see Elisabetta again. She pictured her sleeping on the daybed the way Jill used to when they traveled, her mop of curls heaped on the pillow, falling every which way about her face. How easy it was to please a child: a cup of cocoa, some gelato—a butter dish. Though Jill had been a young woman, there had been times when Joanna could lure her back into the dependency of girlhood, and Jill would allow her mother to pamper her with simple comforts. Joanna brought her coffee into the sunroom and surveyed the countryside. This land grounded her, gave her a sense of identity, of belonging, like an adoptee who had located her birth parents. What did Elliott feel when he came here? It was a lovely land; good roads to hike; great food, but the attachment was missing. She gift-wrapped the woolen throw she had carried across the ocean along with the shiny gold paper, ribbon, and tape. Then she got ready for the party and waited for Elliott to wake.

***

It was a gloriously sunny day, a perfect Easter Sunday that seemed to have burst forth from the gloomy weather of Holy Week like Christ himself from the tomb. The most dangerous kind of day, a day not unlike the one on which Jill had had her accident. A day when you feel nothing can go wrong, that preoccupies you with distractions and makes you forget to take care. A day when everything can be snatched from you.

They walked up the stony drive toward her aunt and uncle's peach stucco home, politely exchanging holiday greetings with several guests they didn't know. They passed the olive grove, and Joanna remembered how on the last trip here with Jill, they had all helped her uncle with the harvest. They had placed nets beneath the trees and carefully hand-picked or raked the olives from the branches, then they gathered them into sacks and brought them into the cantina, where, covering the ground-level room like a rich black carpet, they were left to dry before being taken to be pressed. Jill's new sneakers had gotten coated with mud, and Joanna's aunt tried to clean them with a hand brush and a basin of soapy water. The stains remained, but neither Joanna nor Jill cared. They felt they had earned the bottles of Umbrian olive oil—the best Italy has to offer, according to Joanna's uncle—that they would take back home.

The cantina now held two long tables that stretched the room's entire length, with enough canapés and cakes on them to feed 100 guests, though only about 40 were delicately picking at the array. Joanna placed her gift, which now seemed paltry compared to the others, on the table where unwrapped presents like those of a young bride were displayed: sets of ornately decorated demitasse cups, white satin sheets, silver vases, enormous majolica flower pots—all worthy of a couple starting out. Her aunt, tall and slim with her hair recently permed and brightened with a silver rinse, wore a black suit with a white blouse. Black because it was fashionable, or black because that's what elderly Italian women wore? Black because she only had one good suit, or black because she could not allow herself to be too happy because she was still in mourning? Her uncle, a few inches shorter than her aunt and heavier, had also donned a black suit with a white shirt. With his full head of white hair and unlined olive complexion he was a younger copy of Joanna's father. The Ficola men aged well, Joanna thought. *"Mannaggia!"* they said, hugging and kissing her and shaking her shoulders, cupping her face in their hands. *"Mannaggia!"* That's what they always said when they first saw her. We can't believe that you've come, that you're here! It's like a dream!

"So much time has gone by since your last visit," her uncle said.

"Yes," she said, somewhat apologetically.

"You know that we understand. Everything. You know that."

"Yes."

"You know how sorry we are for you and Elliott. For my brother and his wife."

"I know. Thank you." Her eyes became teary and she needed to change the subject, but he wouldn't let her.

"It takes time, *carissima*. And even then, there is not enough time in all the world. You understand?"

She nodded, hot with discomfort, though she loved him more than ever at that moment. "But today is your day—yours and my aunt's," she insisted.

"Yes. Today is a happy day. I won't see many more days like this one."

Finally they were past it. It was over. Her uncle turned to greet other guests.

"Take it easy," she reminded Elliott as he filled his plate. "Pace yourself. You know what's coming."

When everyone left for the church, she looked back at the table crammed with food that her cousins and aunt had worked all week to prepare. It appeared untouched.

***

With a children's choir singing the praises of a risen Christ, her aunt and uncle renewed their vows during the Mass. They did not leave the church with the briskness of newlyweds, however, as they tottered on arthritic legs, arms linked, each supporting the other. Classical music was piped out into the piazza as they stood at the portal and were congratulated by the townspeople. The priest climbed onto his motorcycle and sped off toward the mountaintop monastery where he lived by himself in what her uncle liked to call selfish hypocrisy. But today her uncle did not vent his disdain for the clergy: today was a joyous day, and the aromas—the *profumo* of simmering tomato sauce and browning roast—wafted down the long flights of steps lined with pots of red geraniums, stimulating their appetites for the long meal that would follow. Elliott took her hand as they strolled with the others to the restaurant. She squeezed it, and he smiled with gratitude.

The guests sat in two long rows and the waiters came by again and again, filling their plates with *crostini, prosciutto, formaggio, fettucine* with tomato sauce, the wider *pappardelle* with truffles, several servings of green vegetables, one of roasted potatoes, chicken, pork, beef, rolled veal, salad, and finally the cream-filled wedding torte. Joanna translated the surrounding conversations that were beyond Elliott's grasp.

Her uncle gave a speech about his wife of 50 years, a woman whose strength and patience with him had helped their marriage endure. He could have said more about her, Joanna thought. She was an amazing woman who after the war had been forced to live in a shed with a dirt floor and who had cared for Joanna's grandparents until their deaths. He thanked his guests for coming, and he acknowledged that Joanna and Elliott had traveled such a long distance. His greatest praise was reserved for his new daughter-in-law, the woman who had married his son-in-law after Joanna's cousin Alessandra had died of cancer several years before Jill's accident.

Suddenly, the 15 courses were churning in Joanna's stomach; the room became hot and stuffy; and she wanted to be anywhere else. She told Elliott she was going to the ladies' room, but when she left the hall, she walked past it and out the door. Standing across the piazza, she moved down a dark narrow street whose buildings seemed to lean inward to keep out the threatening unknown: the cars, the tourists, the sun that made them much more vulnerable. She emerged into the light again, passing a new two-story apartment complex in what had once been considered the outskirts. Crossing the road, she mounted a hill and imagined herself an ant crawling up the head of a bald man who might at any moment sneeze and fling her off. At length she reached the place where they were all buried: her grandparents, her great-grandparents, and her cousin Alessandra.

Her uncle had put his parents underground but had built a grand mausoleum for his daughter. It was white marble, with a large stained-glass image of Jesus exposing his pained sacred heart above the double brass doors. Elongated stained-glass angels on the narrow sidelights stood guard. Joanna peeked in as best she could through a clear pane between the angels' wings: spaces for five more coffins awaited; a broom rested in the corner of a spotless marble floor. A large urn of fresh flowers on a pedestal in the opposite corner indicated that the tomb had been visited recently, and yet her uncle had spoken about his new daughter-in-law without shedding a tear. Even her aunt had forced a smile. Could they possibly have found a replacement for Alessandra? The amount of time it would take to get over a loss like this didn't exist, her uncle had told her himself. And yet they had found a way to go on.

Life was all about loss, a psychiatrist she'd seen after Jill's death intoned, rattling off items as though reading a grocery list: job, property, homeland, a beloved, health, youth, beauty, money, reputation, self-esteem, confidence, desire, a mind. Life was about learning to do without. But sometimes it was possible to recoup one's loss, wasn't it? Sometimes it was only a matter of remembering where you'd deposited your treasure, finding that it had just taken a short vacation from you and mutated itself into a new form. Sometimes you rediscovered it hidden beneath a rock or a pile of dirty laundry, right under your nose.

She didn't know how long she sat there, but when she returned to the restaurant, the guests were pouring out. Elliott met her, his eyebrows raised.

"That was one hell of a pee," he said.

"Sorry."

"I've had to put off people who noticed you were gone. Luckily, they don't expect me to understand their questions."

"I'm sorry. Really."

"You all right?"

"Better than that."

They returned to the house with the rest of the family and dug into the leftovers from the morning.

"How do we do this?" she asked, meaning the marathon eating.

"I don't know, but I'm glad you do," Elliott said, filling a paper plate and pouring some Chianti into a plastic cup.

"We'll see you tomorrow for lunch," her aunt announced as they said their goodbyes.

Her family clung to her like a dog that has taken the seat of your pants between his teeth. Elliott got the gist of the familiar conversation, and his reaction pulled Joanna to the opposing corner.

"We're heading to Rome for a few days," Joanna said.

"You come all this way for one day?" her aunt said.

"We really don't have much time this trip."

"For breakfast then. On your way out."

Be strong, Elliott's eyes said. Hang tough. Remember, it's all an act.

Joanna hesitated.

"But you have to eat," her aunt persisted gracefully, defying resistance.

"For lunch," Joanna conceded.

Both her aunt and Elliott broke into grins, hers of victory, his, politeness. Now it was Joanna who seemed eager to leave. There were things she needed to discuss with Elliott, so many plans to make.

***

Paolo's car was gone when they arrived back at the villa. In their apartment, Elliott moved from behind her, as she began to undress, nuzzling his face against her cheek. He smelled like her father's wine cellar.

"Have a good time?" he asked.

"Elliott, I want to stay here."

"Yeah. It's a neat place. Wasn't it a good idea of mine? Next time we'll stay longer. But we've got three days at a pretty cool hotel in Rome."

"No. I mean I want to stay here."

"You don't want to go to Rome?"

"I don't want to go home."

He lifted his head, and she turned to face him. "We could move here, Elliott. I could work with Paolo. He needs someone like me who speaks English. And you could find work, I'm sure of it. They'd be thrilled to have an American doctor."

"First of all, that's not as easy as you think, but that's beside the point. Why now? We've talked about spending time here when we retire. Why now?"

"It's Jill, Elliott. I know it. I see it in Elisabetta's eyes, I feel it when I touch her. I dreamt about Jill last night. She was little again, and she had Elisabetta's face. I understood it at the cemetery today. Alessandra was telling me, Jill, all the dead. And I can't leave her."

Joanna had sat there on the rocky hill amidst them, straining in the silence, begging for a sign, wishing for a sudden fierce wind or a miraculous deluge out of sunny skies to bring her confirmation—something. Where was the wisdom that came from having met death, and what good was it, if not to serve the living? Yet they had smugly remained mute—all of them—as though honoring some code of silence: "We know; you have to find out for yourself." But when the silence had reached a deafening crescendo, she heard them—daughter, cousin, grandmother, townspeople—all chanting in affirmation. "Yes," they echoed. "Yes."

Elliott was silent for a moment. He took a deep breath and exhaled; he was losing his patience with her.

"This is the only place you can be happy? Here with this child? Who, by the way, is not Jill. And even if she were, as you believe, Jill reincarnated, she's not ours, Joanna. She belongs to somebody else."

"But we can be part of her life, Elliott. We can watch her grow. I can teach her things. I can help her not to make mistakes. Look, her mother's still a child herself. Elisabetta needs me, Elliott. She needs both of us. And I do believe she's Jill. She was born three days after Jill died. Jill's spirit chose this baby's body, Elliott."

"Three days? What took her so long?"

"You're despicable when you joke like that."

"I'm not joking, I'm incredulous. Look, Joanna, I understand you want a second chance to protect Jill, believe me. But if you actually mean what you're saying, I feel sorry for you."

"I don't want your pity."

"Then what do you want?"

"You said you'd give me time. You said whatever it took."

"It's been almost four years! Four years, Joanna! I can't continue like this. We're growing farther and farther apart. You do nothing to ease my pain. You do nothing to help me go on with you. Jill died. We didn't." His eyes welled up.

"There are times I can feel her slipping away. Times when I laugh or begin to enjoy myself, and she's out of my thoughts for a second, and I hate myself."

"How do you think I feel? I'm an ER doc, and I couldn't save my own daughter's life when I found her lying there. How do you think it feels to live with that? One thing you've probably been right about is the eating—the sublimation part. But it's time for us to wake up before it's too late. This is our life now, Joanna. I don't know how else to say it. This is our life."

"I hated the speech my uncle gave today. That's why I had to walk out. I hated the part about thanking Cristina for taking Alessandra's place. But at the cemetery I began to understand. They had to find a replacement—a reminder, a way not to forget."

"Do you think Alessandra is ever out of their thoughts? This is it, isn't it? You're afraid you'll forget Jill."

"Sometimes I miss her so much I think I'll go crazy, then other times it's as though she's away at college the way she used to be. That's all, away for a while. She'll be back again for the holidays. And it's fine. And I catch myself, and I hate myself."

He dug his fingers into her arms and looked at her squarely.

"Listen to me, Joanna. Listen to what I'm telling you. It's okay to be happy. You won't forget her. We can never forget. She was our baby. But we need to live for each other. Look at me, Joanna. See me. Love me."

"We could adopt her. We could give her a better life than Domenica can."

"For Chrissake, we're in Italy, not Ethiopia!"

"People do it in the States."

"People who decide to give up their children at birth. You haven't heard a damn thing I've said, have you?"

She laughed and conceded that her idea was absurd. She threw her arms around him and held him tight. She kissed his forehead, his nose, his lips. She would make love to him tonight. She would see him the way he wanted to be seen. Or at least he would think she did.

***

She took her cappuccino and *cornetto* alone in the dining room early the next morning while Elliott showered. When Domenica and Elisabetta arrived, she presented the child with a colorful beaded necklace of hers, something she had picked up from a beach vendor in the Bahamas. She put it around Elisabetta's neck and told her to go to the mirror in the bathroom and see how beautiful she looked. While she was gone, Joanna made her pitch.

"*Ma Lei è pazza!*" Domenica screamed, stepping back from the crazy lady.

Paolo came running from the kitchen into the foyer. "What is it? What's happening?"

"She's mad!" Domenica's eyes were wide with fear. "She wants to take Elisabetta to America!"

"What are you saying?" Paolo asked Domenica.

"Tell him. Tell him what you said." She recoiled even further from Joanna.

"Is this true, signora?" he asked.

Elisabetta came skipping into the room but was quickly shielded by Domenica.

If Joanna could just touch this little girl, make that physical connection, the child would realize where she belonged. They would all realize. Paolo had said it: at Villa Foresta, all things were possible. Joanna grabbed Elisabetta by the hand and ran outdoors, toward the parking lot. It was mother against mother.

At the stairs that led to the parking lot, Joanna swept the child into her arms and started down. She could hear them behind her—a cacophony of shouts growing louder. That's when Joanna lost her footing. She tried to hold on to Elisabetta, but the girl rolled away from her, as though she'd been snatched out of Joanna's arms. Joanna went to get up, but her foot was entangled in something. "Elisabetta!" she cried, like a wounded animal in a trap.

That was all she remembered.

***

She awoke to the smell of antiseptic cleansers. A man in a green jumpsuit was sweeping a rag over every inch of the stretcher next to her.

"This wouldn't fly in the States," Elliott said. "You can't sanitize a room with a patient in it." He was sitting beside her, holding her hand.

"What kind of a hospital is this?" she asked.

"Don't worry. I haven't committed you. Although I can't say I didn't think about it. I wanted to get a scan. You were out for about ten minutes. I put you in the car and whisked you down here to Terni. To tell you the truth, I was hoping you wouldn't wake up until we were the hell out of there. Or at least I was hoping you had the sense to fake it. They were about to call the police on you, and I can't say I blame them. And there I was, like a mute, unable to explain your 15 minutes of insanity. You've been waking up on and off. Your head took a good bang when it hit the ground. You have a mild concussion, but nothing some peace and quiet won't cure."

"Is my ankle broken?"

"Your ankle's fine."

"I got it caught in some vines on the steps."

"No, you didn't."

"I must have."

"You weren't caught in anything. There aren't any vines on those steps; they're concrete, busted concrete. You just tripped."

"I got tripped, Elliott, and I couldn't free myself. Something had me in its grip."

"Okay, take it easy. You're supposed to stay calm. Fine. You got tripped. Short-term memory is usually jarred by concussions."

"Elisabetta? Was she hurt?"

"Not a scratch."

"What about my aunt and uncle? We were supposed to be there for lunch."

"I found a nurse who speaks some English. She called them for me and said that you'd had a little accident and that we'd used up all our time at the hospital. She told them we needed to get on to Rome—on with our lives ..." His voice trailed off.

"That must have gone over big. They'll hear about it, you know. News spreads like wildfire around these small towns."

"Look, try to stay awake so I can get you discharged as soon as possible."

"Keep talking to me, Elliott. Just keep talking."

"That usually puts you to sleep." He smiled.

"Elliott, maybe I didn't get tripped. Maybe I just got tired and couldn't run anymore. Maybe—" She fought the heaviness of her eyelids. "Maybe I let her go."

***

As they drove past a field of poppies, she thought about her thawing garden back home. The daffodils would surely be blooming when they returned. Tulips would follow. Perennials were faithful that way. No matter how you neglected them, they never abandoned you. The storm clouds gathered on the horizon, signaling the new tempest Elliott and she were about to enter as they drew nearer to Rome. He could think her mad—they could all think her mad. Wasn't that a natural consequence of losing a child? And it could pour every day for all she cared; that would keep the treasure she carried from Villa Foresta safe. After all, Paolo had said it: thieves never steal in the rain.

They entered the dark mountain tunnel and her usual feeling of panic washed over her. She gripped Elliott's thigh; he placed his hand over hers and kept it there until the daylight drew them out. This time he didn't speak. At the entrance to the *autostrada*, she went for the bag of trail mix and held it out to him, but he put up his hand like a crossing guard and shook his head.

Deluxe Meatloaf

"Sorry I'm late, honey." Rosemary was a ball of energy, never coming up for air. "Was this the only seat? Did you ask? I hate sitting in the middle of a restaurant like this. I really don't feel like seeing anyone tonight. I'd rather hide in our little corner by the kitchen."

"I didn't ask for another seat," Nate said.

"Why not?"

"Because I just didn't. It wasn't that important."

"To you."

"Look, Rosie, you're the one with the secret identity. Everyone knows who I am."

"Lots of people know who I am."

"Are we going to start counting names?" Nate asked.

"I'm too hungry. Let's order first." She opened her menu and scanned the pages.

"I already did."

She looked up surprised. "How come?" she asked.

"I don't know. I just felt like it. I've been sitting here for some time."

"I hope you told the waiter not to bring your meal until mine came."

"He'll get the idea."

"What did you order?"

"The usual," he said. "Two Lovers."

"I don't feel like shrimp tonight."

"You didn't order it. I did."

"But we always share, Nate."

"Well, we don't have to tonight."

"What bug's up your ass?"

The couple across the aisle turned their heads to get a look at the woman with the dirty mouth in the jeans and white pullover sitting across from the man in the gray pin-striped suit, white shirt, and red tie.

"Mind lowering your voice? Nothing like not wanting to be noticed." Nate took a sip of his margarita.

Rosemary laughed. It was throaty like a smoker's laugh.

"I don't know why you insist on drinking margaritas with Thai food," she said. "Margaritas are for Mexican food."

"What does it matter? They're both spicy foods. Would it make you feel better if I called it a *loi krathong*?"

"Is that Thai for margarita?"

"No, it's some Buddhist holiday I read about that they celebrate in Thailand."

"I'll have a *loi krathong*, please," Rosemary told the waiter, who had approached the table pen and pad in hand.

Nate shook his head in disbelief. The waiter furrowed his brow.

"Just kidding. A glass of Chardonnay, please. And a tom yum soup, and the pad thai with chicken. You can bring it all at once." She closed her menu with the finality of finishing a five-hundred-page novel.

"Did I embarrass you?" she asked Nate.

"I stopped taking responsibility for my wife's actions a long time ago."

"That's a good answer. I should jot that down for my column."

"I probably got it from your column."

***

When Nate had phoned that afternoon, Rosemary had been answering her favorite letter of the day, one that would surely make it into her column:

> *Dear Lydia,*
> *I'm fourteen and would like to be able to talk to my mother about sex, but I can't bring myself to say anything. She's never brought up the subject. Do you know what would make it easier for me to open up to her? I have a steady boyfriend and need to make some decisions very soon. Please help before it's too late.*
>
> *Too Shy in Torrington*

(Of course she wasn't Lydia. Lydia had choked on the olive in her daily martini ten years before. No one had suspected that she was 82 until the obituary appeared, because she had used the same photograph for 50 years on the column syndicated to 23 small New England newspapers. When Rosemary was asked to become the new Lydia, she was told that she could change neither the picture nor the name.)

Rosemary had suggested that the troubled teenager prepare meatloaf for her tired working mother. Even if the mother didn't work, she was a bad cook, Rosemary was certain. This was about building courage and self-esteem —confidence. If she could whip up a meatloaf with roasted potatoes, peas, and a salad, she could approach her mother about any subject. Meatloaf was perfect, a comfort food that could be prepared by a novice with relative ease. She attached her recipe for Deluxe Meatloaf to her e-mail response.

Maybe tonight Rosemary would make meatloaf herself, she had thought. Nate loved meatloaf—hers, that is. His mother's meatloaf had been one giant burnt hamburger. That had been Thursday's meal. The other days of the week she had turned out something equally bland and over-cooked: gristly steak on Sunday, spaghetti with ketchup on Monday, broiled-to-death chicken on Tuesday, salt-en-crusted cod on Wednesday, and cold pizza delivered on Friday. The chicken reappeared on Saturday. The same menu was repeated every week. She considered fresh vege-tables too much trouble, so she boiled canned peas for twenty minutes to feel, Rosemary guessed, as though she was really cooking. Yes, today would have been a good cold day to turn on the oven and bake a meatloaf, but then Nate called to suggest dining out.

"It was going to be meatloaf—one of your favorites," she had told him.

"It's all my favorite."

"With mashed potatoes."

"I'd really like to go out."

"Got a yen for something?"

"Anything. I don't really care."

"So why do we have to go out?"

"You know, most women would love for their husbands to take them out."

"Okay. Okay."

"Let's meet at The King of Siam," he suggested.

She had read a few more pleas for advice that would not appear in the column but to whose authors she provided swift and logical plans of action nevertheless: A happens and you do B; B happens and you do C. You cut yourself; you bleed. You commit certain actions; you take responsibility for them. To quote her mother, it was all *bel e chiaro*—nice and clear, neat and tidy. People made messes of their lives because they couldn't simplify; they couldn't see what was coming next. Blanch off the skin, trim the fat, skim the grease, clarify the stock, boil it down—reduce!

If people only lived their lives the way they cooked, they would find their burdens much lighter. But that was another problem: people didn't cook anymore, couldn't even follow a recipe, and the majority of counselors were telling them that it was okay in this busy world; in fact, it was necessary for survival. Boy, did they have it wrong. Family mealtime had become as archaic as tea aprons wrapped around shirtwaist dresses.

She had been covering the police log at the local paper, where she was notorious for giving advice to lovelorn young reporters, when she was recruited for the column. Her instant success came as no surprise to her friends and family. As far back as college, Rosemary had been the Dr. Joyce Brothers of Lyndon Hall—the guru of heartbreak, of parental discord, of misunderstandings between roommates. But Rosemary remained convinced that her secret lay in the fact that she provided a recipe in many of her responses. The volume of pleas for help was so great that she couldn't give a recipe with every answer, so it became a lottery of sorts. It was like having the discount gold coin drop from the cash register into the cashier's hand at the grocery store, or like being the millionth customer to walk into the car dealership and be rewarded with a new SUV. Since everyone wanted a recipe, readers competed to pose the week's most desperate, saddest or complicated problem. In truth, Rosemary had no system for selection; she merely had an instinct about the neediest cases—a gut response. It was, she believed, the act of nurturing that was missing in their lives.

Most of the recipes had been handed down from her grandmother and mother, while some dishes Rosemary concocted herself. She never ran out, since friends and family were always sending her ones they thought fit for a grieving widower or a wife with a gay husband. What really mattered was the act of preparation: the chopping, the sautéing, the stirring, the inhaling, and above all the caring, and the satisfaction of fulfillment.

"You are an artist," she told her readers.

The idea to include a recipe came from her Aunt Vita who had worked in a women's clothing store and who on one occasion had deftly handled a most difficult customer. A woman who had been scorned by her husband enjoyed unleashing her rage on the staff and the shop owner. Aunt Vita convinced the woman that her husband left her after she had stopped cooking gourmet meals in a misguided weight-loss program. In denying her husband good food, she had denied him love itself. Aunt Vita ended her lecture by writing down a recipe for *osso buco* for the woman to lure her husband back. The woman left the store high as a kite, and Vita's boss gave her a promotion. Rosemary had concluded that her Aunt Vita was a genius.

Then there was Nate, who thought he'd died and gone to heaven when he was invited to spend Christmas Eve with the Ficolas. He'd heard about the seven fishes Italians ate on The Eve, as they called it, but he'd never imagined the feast that would be set before him. Never mind seven fishes—there must have been 70, each prepared a different way. He proposed to Rosemary on Christmas morning.

He was a man with appetites, and Rosemary knew how to satisfy them. Though a clean and beautiful home, good conversation and a weekly paycheck were all very nice, sex and food was the glue that held their marriage together, the staples Nate couldn't live without. And while middle age had dulled the frequency of the former, the certainty of a healthy and creative meal every day, she knew, sustained him now more than ever. Providing good food to those one loved was, perhaps, the greatest gift of self.

When early in their marriage, Nate used to work late hours, Rosemary never failed to eat with her children at the normal dinner time and discuss the day's happenings. A colorful plateful (indicative of a balanced meal) covered with waxed paper and ready for the microwave awaited Nate upon his return home. In fact a dish still waited for him these days, when he couldn't finish his paperwork or avoid evening meetings.

***

"Julia called me today. She has another exam tomorrow. That makes 25, and she's not even midway through the semester."

Rosemary took a sip of her Chardonnay.

"Med school's not like college," Nate said. "I got a text from Thomas today."

"What's new?"

"He's about to take another group rafting down the Colorado. Maybe someday he'll get a real job."

"He has a real job. It makes him happy."

The waiter delivered their meals, and Rosemary wasted no time digging in. Nate, on the other hand, pushed the food around with his fork.

"I really wish they had chopsticks here," he said.

"They don't usually use chopsticks in Thailand."

"We're not in Thailand. Besides, some Thai restaurants have chopsticks."

"Only for the culturally confused like you, Nate."

"And what about us? Are we confused?"

Nate asked that question with such regularity that Rosemary accepted the tedious dialogue that usually lifted him out of his doldrums as dutifully as the discomfort of her annual mammogram. It was always his needs that weren't being met. Poor frustrated Nate. After they'd gone around in circles and she'd either convinced him that he was too demanding or promised to make a few changes, she usually steered the conversation in the direction of their retirement or vacation plans and ended it on a more upbeat note.

Tonight, however, she was a little surprised, since they had made love that morning, and lovemaking usually put him in a good mood for a few days. He worked too hard, and he was getting older and wearier. Just a few more years until Julia graduated, and then he could stop. And her? Maybe she'd take on an assistant. Yes, that would be the way to go, because she wasn't ready to kick the bucket like dear old Lydia, even figuratively. She was kind of tired herself tonight, so she skipped over the messy stuff and headed straight for the happy ending.

"I know you want to go to Australia this spring, but I was thinking we could extend the vacation and go to Italy too. My cousin Joanna discovered a great villa."

"I couldn't take that kind of time." He put down his fork and took a large gulp of his margarita.

"You've worked so hard to bring the company to where it is, and it's only made more work for you."

"That's why it'd be nice if Thomas came into the business."

"You had no interest in your father's business."

"That's because my father was a pain in the ass. You know I couldn't work with him."

"What makes you so sure Thomas could work with you?"

The hurt look on his face brought her up short.

"I'm kidding. Look, he just needs to do his own thing. Who knows? Maybe in time he'll want to sell insurance. You can hang on for a few more years, can't you?"

He didn't answer.

"Well?"

"Rosemary, there's something I have to tell you." He stared down at the table.

"Sounds serious." She put a forkful of pad thai into her mouth. Her attempt to lighten the heavy part hadn't worked.

"I've been seeing someone else," he said in a low voice.

She stopped chewing. She wanted to spit the noodles out but opted to swallow them fast. She had to get rid of them.

"Another woman?"

"I feel terrible about it, but I've been warning you for years."

"You've been seeing her for years?"

"No, no. Only about five months. But I want to move in with her."

"What?"

"I'm in love with her."

"Who?"

"Just a woman I met at Dunkin' Donuts, believe it or not." He laughed at the absurdity of it. "She's a teacher. Not in our school system."

"I'm so relieved," she said sarcastically. "You let things get this far without saying anything to me? No marriage counselor?"

"Oh please, Rose. I've suggested seeing someone a million times but you always say we don't need one. You think you can fix everything with meatloaf."

"We'll go to counseling."

"I don't want to anymore."

"Nate, I don't understand. We've always talked."

"I'm tired of talking, Rose. I'm tired of saying the same things. I'm all talked out. And I know I can't spend another 27 years like this."

"Like what? What's so awful about your life?"

"I need someone who wants to be with me."

"And what do you think I've been doing all these years? Killing time until someone else came along? I guess you were."

"Of course I wasn't. But I need more. I've always needed more."

"Fuck you! How old is she?"

"Thirty-two," he mumbled.

"Married?"

"Never been."

"Fuck you!"

"I understand that you're angry."

"Oh, do you? And what about the kids?"

"They're not kids anymore. They'll handle it."

"Then you tell them. You tell them everything."

There were beads of sweat on her upper lip; her underarms were soaked. Heat rose until her whole face felt on fire. An emotional reaction often triggered this these days, but she wouldn't, she would not, pick up the napkin and fan herself the way she usually did. Nate always said it didn't help to do that. How did he know? When was the last time he had a hot flash? She would not give him the satisfaction now; she would not show him her vulnerability.

He was talking, but his voice faded into the background as other voices took over. *Rosemary Ficola Jasinsky, this is your life, and it has just been erased,* a man said. *You didn't want to marry an Italian? You didn't want a mama's boy?* her mother chimed in. *Well mamas' boys stick around home. Then Do over!* Her childhood voice called, pleading for a second chance, as though she had been cheated in a game of hopscotch. Her stomach muscles tightened, and she fought the pad thai's desire to find its way back up her throat. Every day she dished out advice, confident that she possessed the recipe for holding everything together. For the first time in her life, she was speechless.

"I know how you must feel, turning 50 and all. But you'll be okay. You're a strong woman, Rosemary. I've always admired you for that. Though I have to admit I was afraid you'd throw a glass of water in my face."

That's why he had sat in the middle of the restaurant, in front of everyone, the coward.

Rosemary wouldn't remember what she did next: pushing back her chair and standing up, putting on her jacket and gloves, slipping her purse strap over her shoulder, lifting the edge of the black Formica table and tipping it onto Nate's lap. (It was lighter than she'd ever imagined.) She seemed to float out of the restaurant, though she could hear the clicking of her boot heels on the sidewalk like the tick-tock of a grandfather clock or, better yet, a cooking timer counting down the minutes until the marriage was done. Click. Click. Click. She had to stop the sound. She turned into an alley, bent over, and threw up 26 years.

A Perfect Father

There were few unoccupied seats when Nancy boarded the train at Tende, where she'd been visiting her old college friend Judith. The passengers were mostly Italians who must have gotten on at Cuneo or Torino, across the border, and like herself, were headed to Nice.

An elderly gentleman took the precious window seat in the first row of the car. Nancy claimed the aisle one alongside him. She didn't mind traveling backward the way her husband, Jean-Georges, did. However, Jean-Georges never came with her on this annual sojourn during their vacations in France; he preferred to stay with his family at their summer home in Nice. Across from the old man sat a young businessman with wire-rimmed glasses, who tightly gripped the handle of the attaché case that rested on his lap; his large valise in the seat opposite Nancy completed the little foursome. He could have put his suitcase on the luggage rack above, but he left it there as though it were entitled to the seat, as though it had purchased its own ticket. Nancy crossed her legs and accidentally tapped his, which he immediately withdrew as he turned his head to stare out at the countryside. The old man rested his head against the window and fell asleep.

At the next stop, Saint Dalmas de Tende, a man, most likely in his mid-30s, entered the car carrying a paper bag in one hand and guiding a little boy with the other. Quickly, he scanned the car. Then, in a very determined manner and without asking permission, he placed the large suitcase in the aisle and settled the boy into the seat. The businessman seemed about to protest, but the new arrival's actions made it clear that his son would occupy the seat. Nancy smiled. The man across from her pursed his lips and returned his gaze to the window. The father crouched next to the small boy, whose legs stuck straight out because they were too short to bend.

He was a big boy for his age, but Nancy had been an elementary school principal long enough to comfortably estimate him to be around three. He was a happy boy, at least he was happy to be there with his father, whom he resembled, with a round face, eyes like large black olives, and plump skin—not fat but meaty like sausage in its casing. The boy was lighter in skin tone with brown hair. One might first assume that they were Italians: they were unlike the man opposite Nancy, who based on appearance alone—auburn hair, fair skin, pointed nose—would have been taken for a Frenchman. The businessman, however, had used his cell phone to speak to an associate in Italian, while the father addressed his son in French. But then, many of the French in these towns looked Italian and the Italians French, since they lived in an area that had changed ownership again and again at the whims of rogues, land barons, and kings.

The father worked hard to keep his son entertained as the train made its way down the snowcapped mountains of the Maritime Alps, and the child's smile never faded. That made the boy ever so endearing, because it was a genuine smile, eager and full of appreciation, one that could belong only to an individual who was experiencing such a ride for the first time. Clearly secure and content, his good disposition never waned even for a moment. He was the type of child you wanted to hug and take home, to give hot chocolate and cookies to, because it would be impossible to spoil him. Some children are good-natured from the moment they emerge from the womb.

The father performed something like "Itsy Bitsy Spider" with his hands and then did a magic trick, making a coin disappear and reappear. Next, he was a creeping bug climbing the boy's leg, threatening to and then succeeding in tickling the child's stomach. The boy's body convulsed with such delight that several times Nancy laughed out loud, catching the father's eye. The Italian across from her shifted in his seat. The old man began to snore.

How the father's thighs must have ached, crouched as he was at his son's level. Where were they going? To visit *grand-mère*—the father's mother, of course. But just for the day, since they had no luggage. Why wasn't Maman with them? Perhaps she needed time to herself, or was in the last trimester of pregnancy with another child—a girl—and was too tired to make the trip. She was a beautiful woman, Nancy decided: luscious golden tresses like Catherine Deneuve's, slim when she wasn't expecting, blue eyes and a light and clear birdlike laugh. They had grown up together—the mother and father—and fallen in love in grade school. Oh, she hadn't admitted to liking him at first, because he wasn't the cleverest student and always played the prankster, but he had won her over eventually. And he adored her, and had settled down. They weren't rich, but they got by. How proud he was of having won her love, secretly convinced that he didn't deserve it. Her parents, Nancy went on to speculate, had never fully accepted him and often reminded her that she could have done better; but, nevertheless, the husband was tolerant of his in-laws.

A good father. A perfect father. Would Jean-Georges have been capable of such devotion? He had demanded so much attention since she had lured him away from France after her junior year abroad and transplanted him to Boston (unlike her friend Judith, who moved to Torino with the Italian she had fallen in love with). That's why she hadn't insisted on having children: it had seemed the logical and right thing to do—or not to do—all these years, until now, when they were in their early 40s, and Jean-George's failing kidney and her biological clock obviated the decision.

As though it were another magic trick, the father removed a pastry from the paper bag and gave it to the boy, who evidently had a good appetite. He bit off large chunks, yet there was nothing repulsive about his eating habits. On the contrary, Nancy watched him enjoy the pastry with the pleasure a mother feels with a child who eats anything she puts before him.

Her cousin's children, Matthew and Elena, were finicky eaters, while Jill never ate period, and Thomas and Julia would take only what their mother had prepared. The holidays she hosted proved a disappointment. Despite the efforts she put into pleasing the youngsters, Easter biscuits in the shape of birds took nosedives onto the dining room carpet; heart-shaped pink mashed potatoes, carefully arranged on their plates for Valentine's Day, perished of neglect. This boy wouldn't have let them die. This boy would have relished such novelties, his eyes glistening with gratitude.

The boy was still eating when the father motioned something to him that Nancy couldn't make out. The child nodded and the father turned around, opened the door to the foyer between the two cars, and closed the door behind him. He had obviously gone to look for a lavatory, leaving the boy content to munch on his pastry. Nancy wasn't sure she would have left her son alone, had she been fortunate enough to have one; Americans are so paranoid about kidnapping. When she was no more than five, her mother let her walk to the corner store, on the busy avenue, with two quarters wrapped in a shopping list she presented to the grocer. An unthinkable task to assign to a young child nowadays, one that smacked of stupidity, even negligence.

But the boy was safe, really, with all eyes on him (at least Nancy's, of which the father had been well aware). There were always those stories of people stealing children in toy stores and department stores when their mothers had turned their heads for a moment, then whisking the children off to a restroom stall, disguising them in dresses and wigs, and walking out of the store with changed-sex toddlers before any alarm had sounded. Where could one to go with a little boy on a moving train?

Police officers came regularly to Nancy's school and lectured the children on personal safety: what to do if a stranger approached them on their walk home; what to do if their parents failed to pick them up. But this father would be back before the train reached the next station, and one did have to have some faith in human nature. Still, Nancy would assume responsibility for this child until his father returned. She believed she had a tacit understanding with him. Surely, he had taken her for a good woman.

The train rolled along the mountainside. One stiff wind might send it sailing into the ravine, she thought. Of course that never happened, but she liked to fantasize the way her very young students did: sometimes to try to get into their heads, other times because she preferred their creative minds to those of the faculty. In a week, she would be back with them all in Massachusetts. Summer was coming to an end, as was Jean-George's and her time in France.

The train came to a stop, jerked forward, as though it had tripped, and stopped again. The boy looked around, his mouth still holding its cherubic smile. He took another bite of the pastry and settled back into his seat. Nancy looked up at the glass door of the vestibule. The old man's head banged against the window. The man across from her made another business call.

When the train pulled into La Trinité-Victor, the boy looked back at the glass door.

"He's gone to the toilette, right?" Nancy asked in French.

The boy stared, wide-eyed.

"He'll be back soon. The train is very crowded. There must have been a long line."

Maybe he'd met a friend and struck up a conversation, and was on his way back at this very moment; not that much time had passed. The stations were quite close together as they neared the city. Nancy leaned forward.

"What's your name?" she asked

He didn't answer. His parents must have instructed him not to talk to strangers.

Passengers began to gather their belongings: duffle bags, suitcases, and laptops were retrieved from the overhead rack and placed in the aisle. One young woman destined for the beach removed a six-foot inflated yellow float. In an effort to be the first to exit the train when the doors opened, the Italian businessman picked up his attaché case and enormous valise and disappeared behind the glass door. The old man, ignorant of the fact that the boy had a father, since he had been asleep when the pair boarded, awoke promptly as the train pulled into the Nice station.

The boy grew uneasy, his gaze locked on the door behind him as the passengers, standing up, suddenly loomed over him.

"I'll wait with you until your father returns," she assured him.

She crossed over and took the businessman's seat beside the boy. The train began to empty out. When they were the only ones left in the car she said: "Let's go and find him." But the boy, his head turned away from her as he continued to monitor the door, didn't respond. It was at that point she realized he hadn't uttered a word throughout the entire trip and that he might in fact be deaf.

Her overnight bag in one hand, the boy's hand in her other, Nancy set out to look for a conductor. No one had entered their car to punch tickets, but this was not uncommon on this line.

The boy's hand was clammy, the perpetual smile gone, the sparkling eyes stone cold. He skipped to keep up with her as she headed for the group of conductors who were chatting on the platform. They would have to search quickly, before the train filled up again and departed, in all the lavatories, and find the locked door behind which the father would be discovered, collapsed on the floor, deathly ill or worse. Poor man. Should he manage to return to his car before the conductors reached him, all he would find were crumbs on an empty seat.

Nancy gripped the pudgy hand of her new charge as tightly as a coveted prize, anticipation nearly overwhelming her.

"There is no one, Madame," they confirmed as, one by one, they returned. "Your friend is not on the train."

An anxious Jean-Georges smiled when at last he spotted her entering the terminal. He beamed in much in the way an expectant father might have greeted the doctor leaving the delivery room after a difficult labor. And just as the father's relief would have turned to concern while he awaited the news, Jean-Georges' eyes now demanded an explanation for the child walking beside his wife.

It's a boy, she wanted to say.

The Swap

I t was the first day of spring—too cold for swimming, yet the outdoor pool of the Richmond apartment complex was already uncovered. From her ground-level window, Nancy noticed a mallard with his iconic emerald head and gilded beak confidently gliding on the water's surface; the white neckband, like a starched collar against his rich brown chest, gave him the air of a dandy with not a care in the world. "Lucky ducky," Nancy said.

The two-bedroom flat was sparsely furnished; it only needed to see them through five weeks of recovery. Nancy had barely had time to locate the nearest supermarket and stock the kitchen with necessities like coffee and tea, milk and cereal, canned soups, eggs, yogurt, peanut butter, and bread. Until she felt up to cooking, anything more elaborate would have to be delivered. Her mother desperately wanted to come down from Boston to care for her daughter and son-in-law; her cousins said they'd put everything aside to be there for her, but Nancy refused their offers. The strength required for what she was about to do for Jean-Georges must not be susceptible to the anxiety of others and hovered over by nervous hens as though it were a communal incubating egg. On a more selfish note, she did not wish to share this intimate experience between her husband and herself.

Her decision to donate a kidney had been an easy one, for the simple reason that she did not want her life with Jean-Georges to end. But they were incompatible in the scientific sense; in fact, until now no one had qualified to be her husband's donor.

Organ transplanting is a waiting game, and while they had waited for a cadaver donor, Nancy had searched for another option and found a long shot: an in-house swap—a hospital with enough operating rooms, staff and surgical wings to perform multiple exchanges. For many months the hospital worked to find six patients with failing kidneys and six donors who, like Nancy, were incompatible with their relative or friend but compatible with one of the other recipients. Too many cooks spoil the broth, Nancy thought at first; one of them was bound to get the worst doctor, and Nancy feared she'd be the loser. But their choices had evaporated. Jean-Georges was rapidly declining, and they were out of time.

Throughout the process one final obstacle had threatened to stand in the way of the transplant, and in turn, the transplant had threatened to stand in the way of the obstacle. Nancy and Jean-Georges were in the throes of another waiting game: they planned to adopt a child from France—a deaf boy Nancy had found abandoned without identification, on a train in the Maritime Alps. A boy that doctors had determined to be three years and three months old, a boy they had named Pierre.

French adoption authorities had not been perturbed about Jean-George's history of congenital kidney disease, though they were under the impression he was in remission. And if the transplant team in Richmond had known their adoption of a very young child was in the works, they would have eliminated Nancy and Jean-Georges and upset the entire swap project. But it was not the other five people with kidney disease that Nancy had been concerned with; they were, in her eyes, just organs—a means to an end. She had thought only of Jean-Georges and Pierre, and so they decided not to lie about either the adoption or Jean-Georges' health status—depending on whom they were speaking to—but instead to say nothing. A sin of omission.

***

Nancy had never doubted their decision to adopt Pierre until now, the night before their surgeries, as she sat beside her husband on his bed in the apartment that contained no trace of their two decades together. She rested her head against the flimsy wicker headboard that moved each time she did and was enveloped with doubt.

"Are we wrong to go ahead with the adoption? Is it irresponsible?" she asked Jean-Georges. "What if something happens to one of us?"

He was lying face up, eyes closed, in a body aged far older than his 44 years.

"Pierre will be in the best hands with you, should something happen to me. And if it is the other way around, I cannot begin to think about that—but, because you worry, I reassure you that I will be an exemplary father."

"And if something happens to both of us?" They'd been over this numerous times. "I know. If it's after we've gotten him, Joanna will take care of him. And if it's before—he'll be adopted by a French family. I know. I know."

"Nancy, we've looked at this from every angle. Stop torturing yourself."

"Maybe it was wrong from the beginning, Jean. You never wanted children. I pushed you into the adoption."

"I never said I didn't want children. All the rigmarole trying to conceive, all that guilt. You thought that I was too demanding, too needy, but I was trying to make a life with only us in it. I'll get used to this. It's just that it's been the two of us for so long."

"No room. I told myself there was no room for children in a marriage with you. Tell me I was wrong. You'll get used to being a father, won't you?"

"A good father."

"And the fact that he's deaf?"

"I've accepted that. When I saw you come off that train in Nice holding Pierre's little hand, leading him through the crowds, I thought: What has she gone and done now? Promised to babysit someone's child for the rest of our stay in the city? I admit I was a bit jealous. You looked so radiant—happier than I'd ever seen you. I could never make you that happy."

It hurt her to hear him say that, and even more to think it might be true. "I was a nervous wreck. I kept waiting for the father to stab me in the back or for the police to arrest me," she said, adding a note of suspense to the scenario they had visited many times.

"What could you have done? The father disappeared without a trace. We went straight to the police. We gave him up. Relax, *chérie*. Everything will work out. You'll see. Don't be such a pessimist."

"I'm not a pessimist!" she insisted. "I'm a realist. I can't help but see all the possibilities."

"Of what can go wrong." He turned to her: the turquoise eyes that had bewitched her 22 years ago were now ringed with deep shadows accentuated by his sunken cheeks. The grayish pallor of his skin frightened her. He seemed so close to death she could barely look at him. He knew how to slice right through her pretense and expose her fears.

"Nancy, you don't have to do this," he said.

"Don't be an idiot! Of course I'm doing this."

"You have a way with words."

"I'm sorry. But you know I feel absolutely positive about the surgery. I just have dreams of some poor couple showing up at our door one day demanding their child."

"All kinds of records are being checked. All the reports of missing children in the EU. Who knows who or what the mother was, what happened to her. And the father might just have been a sick person, or a desperate person, or a very bad person."

"No, Jean. I don't think he was bad. If you could have seen the way he behaved with the boy: he was so good with him."

"He left him."

"I know. But I can't imagine Pierre having been abused." She shook her head with conviction.

"Well, he was lucky you were on that train. Or maybe he was looking for you—the right person to take care of his son or whatever Pierre might have been to him. You believe in all that fate stuff. I don't. However you view it, you were a treasure the man came upon: a gift in exchange for a gift—an angel. Stop playing both sides of the tennis court and turn off your brain. You're driving me crazy."

"I'm done," she said. "And I'm hungry." Her surgery was scheduled for early morning, and she couldn't have anything in her stomach for eight hours beforehand. She never ate at this hour, yet the thought of not being able to made her aware of her empty stomach. Jean-Georges, on the other hand, who wasn't scheduled until late afternoon, had just finished a large meal and now sipped chamomile tea.

She got off the bed, walked around to his side, and picked up the mug of tea from the nightstand. Wrapping her hands around it, she lifted it to her forehead and held it there.

"I think you missed your mouth," he said.

"I have a headache. The heat helps."

"Maybe you should see a doctor first thing in the morning."

"Funny."

His frail hand floated upward, and he patted her stomach.

"Don't." She waved him away, spilling some of the tea. "I don't like it when you do that. I feel like you're consoling my barren womb. You aren't the only one with a dysfunction."

His hand dropped onto the bed.

"Would you like something else to eat?" She felt bad about snapping at him.

"No. I'm not hungry. Remember the first time we slept together, in Aix, in my parents' bed when they went to the seashore, and I got up afterward and made you a *croque monsieur*, and you were disappointed? 'It's just a grilled cheese sandwich fried in egg,' you said."

"I wasn't disappointed. It was delicious. I just thought it was going to be more exotic. It was my first week in France. Remember how hot it was in that flat way up on the fourth floor? We were so sweaty and thirsty."

"Your first week?" he said. "Did we do it so soon?"

"You know we did."

"Do you regret it?"

"The sandwich or the sex?"

"Having spent your junior year in France. Having met me. Having become a couple so quickly."

"How could I? I was drunk in love from the minute you pronounced my name."

"You just wanted a French boyfriend—an upperclass-man— so you could learn to speak French better."

"Do you regret it? You were young for a man to give up other women."

"I'd love a cigarette right now. That's the only thing you made me give up that I miss. Do you want a man or a woman to get your kidney?"

Nancy hadn't even thought about who was going to receive her kidney; she hadn't thought much about any of the members of the swap, since they were forbidden to know anything about each another. She was in this for her husband's sake, and she viewed the others as a collective means to an end—Jean-Georges' cure.

"I guess it doesn't matter—as long as it isn't a Republican," she said, then giggled.

"You know what I'd really like now even more than a cigarette?"

"What?"

"To make love."

They both knew the impossibility of that, given his weak state. They had not made love in months.

"I knew you were sex crazed the day you cupped my derriere when you walked behind me into the registrar's office in Aix," she told him.

He was looking up at her now, studying her face as though trying to see something he'd never found before.

"Here we go!" He used that expression to confirm that something was true. "That is the day I saw you with your long black hair and eyes and I didn't think you were an American at all. I thought you were from Malta or Tunisia, or a Gypsy from southern Spain, you had such a mysterious air about you. You walked past me and it was like being brushed by a field of strawberries, you smelled so good. I knew right then that I must have you."

"Ere we go," she said, imitating his accent. "Sometimes I think I shouldn't have made you come to the States. Maybe we would have been happier if we had stayed in France."

"Ohlala, you take credit for everything, don't you? It was my decision too."

"But you miss being there."

"I would miss the States if we left. I'm just a malcontent."

"*C'est vrai*," she said.

"You know there's something romantic about having the surgery here," he said.

"You find Richmond romantic?"

"It's my first time here, therefore it's an unknown full of possibilities. Besides, five weeks alone with you and no interruptions is very romantic. I'm going to bring you a *croque monsieur* when it's over."

"And just how are you going to manage that?"

"You'll see. I'll manage." He laughed. "I'm very resourceful."

"We should get some rest. We have to be at the hospital at the crack of dawn." Nancy found herself as excited as a bride on the night of her wedding. "Do you need anything else before I go to my room?"

"Yes. My goodnight kiss."

She bent over and softly kissed him on the lips. She had imagined them cold and hard, but to her relief, they were soft and warm.

"Promise me you won't ever be sorry that we adopted Pierre, if something happens to me," she begged. "I can't help it, but that's the only thing that terrifies me right now. As far as doing this, I've never been surer. I must sound awful asking this of you right now."

"You sound like a mother, that's what you sound like."

"Promise me you won't regret it."

He squeezed her hand as hard as he could, but the weakness of his grip only reinforced her determination to undergo the surgery.

"*Je ne regret rien, ma chérie*," he whispered. He closed his eyes. "There is one more thing I'd like."

"What is it?"

"Stay here tonight. In my bed."

"You'll be able to sleep? It's smaller than our bed at home."

"It's the only way I will."

She went to the other side, slipped under the covers, and snuggled up to him until their bodies were perfectly fitted. She rested her head against his shoulder; he lifted his foot and crossed it over hers.

***

In the morning, Nancy was euphoric about what she was going to do. While they waited for the taxi, she went out to the pool to feed Lucky: she wanted the duck to be there when she returned from the hospital and wished she knew someone she could ask to care for it. As she approached the pool, plastic bag of bread chunks in hand, she was heartened to see that a mottled brown female had joined the drake; she named her Mrs. Lucky. As a couple, they were much more apt to survive.

***

The hospital, normally quiet on a Saturday, was abuzz with excitement, all energy focused on the transplants. Though the staff had performed multiple procedures before, it was the first time a 12-way had happened, and all dozen participants were assembled in a holding area, curtains drawn around each gurney.

It reminded Nancy of how, when she was four years old having her tonsils removed, they had pinned white cloths around the heads of the children in the ward to cover their hair, placed each child on a gurney, and, one by one, taken them up for surgery. She could recall being strapped down and wheeled through the halls, into an elevator, and into a small green operating room, where her doctor's face peered down at her, a round mirror fastened onto a headband. An ether mask was placed over her face; she saw spirals—then blackness. She had been the last to be taken to surgery, and had felt lonely, singled out, scared.

But this morning she was the first to go, right after a young woman drew blood samples and then, with a black marker, made a picture of an angel on her wrist. But she wasn't wheeled into this operating room. In fact, she was told to hop off the gurney and walk.

As she passed the 11 cubicles, terrycloth socks with rubber-gripping soles protecting her feet against the cold linoleum, she could hear the candidates murmuring, and she wanted to pull open each curtain, see their faces, and carry them like a teddy bear into the OR.

"Don't touch anything blue!" they warned her as she stepped into a room so high-tech it resembled a science-fiction spacecraft. They strapped her onto a tablelike contraption. With arms outstretched, immobilized like Christ on the cross, this sacrificial lamb gladly surrendered.

***

A grilled cheese sandwich was waiting on Nancy's bedside tray when she awoke, only the bread was hard and the cheese rubbery from having sat so long. She couldn't tell if it was dusk or dawn.

"I'm sorry," the nurse said, "but your husband gave us strict orders to have it here when you opened your eyes, so we couldn't time it just right. You've been awake and out for hours. He wanted us to find a French bistro and order something called a cock masseuse, but this was the best we could do. It's from the cafeteria."

"Can I see him?"

"If you can get out of bed and into this wheelchair parked outside the door."

The nurse took Nancy for a ride to the ICU, where she was startled to see tubes emerging from every part of Jean-Georges. His hands rested on top of the thin white blanket. He barely opened his eyes when Nancy was wheeled to his bedside.

"Hi," she said.

He forced a smile. She raised a finger and touched the corresponding one of his that held the clothespin-shaped blood oxygen monitor. Looking like the two inebriated lovers in a painting above their mantel at home, their heads slumped and they immediately fell asleep.

***

It didn't take long for the secrecy surrounding the Swap Twelve to begin to unravel. They could be spotted by the way they walked, the black angel on the wrists of some, and by the curiosity in the eyes of those who longed to know which one had been responsible for extending their lives. As the anticipation built, the staff realized that something had to be done, and a meeting was arranged—a multiple blind date of sorts, where partners and recipients and doctors and nurses came together in one room. It was a thanksgiving, a jubilant revelation, a family reunion because from individual concern, a family had been born. There was cake and music, tears and gratitude, hugging and kissing for everyone but Nancy, who, feeling like a high school girl who had been stood up on prom night, couldn't find her recipient, and who, for the first time, was desperate to see and talk to this person within whom part of her now resided.

Then Nancy was led to a room to meet Maggie, still too weak to join the party. And only then did Nancy experience the rush that came with understanding fully what she had done for this fragile woman with red hair and freckles and green eyes, the wife of a pleasant-looking man and mother of a teenage daughter, who both nearly crushed Nancy —their angel—with gratitude, until all four broke down and cried.

"Thank you," Maggie said sobbing.

Nancy took Maggie's hand and, the way a mother examines her newborn, passed her thumb over each of Maggie's slender fingers, observed the upward curve of her nose, the thinness of her dry parted lips. At last she knew how it felt to have given birth—to have given life.

***

When reporters, photographers, and TV crews came to cover the amazing feat, Nancy pretended she was sleeping to avoid being interviewed, fearing that word would reach the French adoption authorities. Relieved when she and Jean-Georges returned to the seclusion of the apartment, she was thrilled to see that not only had Mr. and Mrs. Lucky survived, but there were now 13 ducklings with them. Nancy had never known a duck to have had so many young; she swore they symbolized the 12 members of the swap plus Pierre. She fed them every day—her most ambitious physical exercise—and hoped the weather would not get too warm and bring big hairy humans and noisy kids with inflated alligators and beach balls to run the family out of town.

"I can't cook," she told Jean-Georges. "There's no dishwasher."

"Since when is that a prerequisite for cooking?" He sat in the armchair, feet up on a hassock. The color of the living had already returned to his face.

"I once heard that a woman poached fish in her dishwasher," Nancy said. "She wrapped it in foil and put it through the wash cycle. She just left out the soap."

"You can't be serious."

"I am. But I wouldn't do it. I was insinuating that I can't cook because I don't want to wash the dishes. I can't stand at the sink too long."

"We can use paper."

"Don't get pushy because you're feeling better. Maybe next week. Right now we're still on the soup-and-sandwich plan."

As soon as Jean-Georges was up to it, he and Nancy went down to the pool. They hobbled over to two chaise lounges where, with blankets pulled up to their chins, they read books like a privileged couple of another era crossing the ocean on some luxury steamship.

Thus they went about their adventure of recovery until, healthy enough to make the plane ride home, they packed to leave. They had survived; the adoption was still in progress; they had taken an incredible gamble on all fronts and they had won big-time.

Nancy went out to feed the ducks for the last time, taking extra bread to last them a while. She wished she could leave a dozen loaves and dig them their own private pond, with a shelter and soft hay to sleep on. She wished she could take them home and show them to Pierre, and to her parents and cousins and aunts and uncles.

Approaching the pool in the dark, Nancy confirmed what she thought she had seen from a distance: one of the ducklings was floating motionless in the water. Mrs. Lucky was alone by the pool wall, emitting what Nancy interpreted as a mourning whine, and Nancy knew that something bad was about to happen.

***

The hospital staff didn't wait until Nancy was home and surrounded by her family to call her about Maggie's death. Why would they? They had come to know her well, this proud woman who preferred not to be coddled by nurses and orderlies and aides. The news numbed her like a whole-body epidural. Her perfectly good kidney was not good enough to save her recipient, who had suffered a heart attack. Maggie and her perfectly good kidney were dead.

What a waste! What a fucking waste of a life! she wanted to yell.

"I'm so sorry, Nancy," Jean-Georges said from his bed.

There was no consoling her. She went into the bathroom and scrubbed away the faint traces of the angel she'd been trying to preserve. Most of it had worn off weeks ago, yet she saw it as distinctly as on the day it had been drawn. She felt Maggie's warm hand, the husband and daughter's embrace, the swelling of her own heart with pride. What a waste! she wanted to scream, not caring whether they heard her in the next apartment or in Paris. What a fucking waste! She wanted to sob, but the sorrow was so great nothing came—just a dull aching moan for the delicate woman with the freckled face and the red hair.

***

It's Indian summer in New England, when the lassitude of hot weather lingers into fall and teases one with the notion that it might stay forever. But it never does, Nancy muses as she and Jean-Georges ride to the airport. They are headed to Nice to claim their son and bring him back home.

Nancy observes Jean-Georges, tanned from a summer of rest, sports jacket over his arm, briskly walking through the terminal in a rejuvenated body. He has more energy than she has ever seen in him. He boards the plane with the presence of a diplomat. He chats in French with the flight attendants. He has already assumed his European persona as he prepares to reenter his homeland. Somewhere in midair, he will leave America behind.

She feels no difference within her own body; she functions no better or worse than she did. But every now and then her thoughts turn to Maggie, and she remembers she's lost something. It comes in a little wave. It might be instigated by something she's read or heard. I have only one kidney, she thinks to herself. But then it goes away.

The Birthing Room

"**D**id you charge the battery in the video camera?" Barbara asked Lenny as she pulled a lavender silk blouse over her head, careful not to mess her makeup or muss her recently highlighted hair.

"Earth to Barbara: My phone videotapes. So does everyone else's." He was leaning in the doorway of the dressing room, watching her as though he hadn't seen her half naked since the first night they made love 20 years ago.

"I want real photos too."

"I'll print the stills and you'll have your photos."

"You'll forget and your party will forever be on a thumbnail or whatever you call it."

"It's a ThumbDrive. Maybe you'd prefer some daguerreotypes."

"That would be so cool, Lenny."

"You were born in the wrong century."

"Someday the kids will appreciate the history I'm leaving them."

"They appreciated the in-home movie theater I had built for them more." He was gloating. "By the way, thanks for doing this."

"We couldn't let your 60th birthday go by like any other day".

"We could have had it at a restaurant. This is so much work for you."

"We have this big house, and everybody loves coming here. Don't you think so, Lenny? Don't they like coming to our house? My cousins will help. Besides, what else have I got to do now?"

"You think it's so great out there?" he said. "You're lucky you don't have to work. I know tons of women who would give their eyeteeth not to have to."

Her temples pulsated with the mere thought of their life after the twins, Matthew and Elena, left for college in the fall. She longed to be pregnant again, to feel productive 24 hours a day. Working while she was carrying the twins had been like putting in overtime.

"You're my Martha Stewart." He slipped a black silk sports jacket over his black cashmere turtleneck.

Comparing her to the woman whose domestic skills had built a megabucks empire did little to mitigate her fears of the impending empty nest and her regret for having let her school librarian certification expire long ago. She did love the idea of the party, however, the planning, the decorating, and preparing the food that would make her guests ooh and aah and stuff themselves. The party had occupied her from morning to night. Friends would be arriving soon, and her family was coming from Massachusetts. Yes, the party had provided the perfect outlet for her at a most vulnerable time.

"I don't know why you didn't tell people not to bring gifts. I don't need anything except for the Dow to keep climbing," Lenny said, running a comb through his curly gray hair and smiling with approval into the full-length mirror Barbara had abandoned. He patted the bald spot at the back of his crown.

"No one will notice it if you don't sit down, since you're taller than most of the guests," she told him. "By the way people don't believe it when you tell them not to bring presents. They just agonize more over whether or not they should bring a little something because they're afraid they'll be the only ones who listened and came empty-handed."

"See what I mean. You're the wise one."

"I hate when you patronize me, Lenny."

"It's supposed to rain tonight. Hard."

"Can you put the old carpet out in the front hall? Please," she added softening her take-charge tone.

Lenny didn't like to be talked down to. He was in the habit of advising wealthy clients, albeit on financial matters only. The house was Barbara's domain. She couldn't let water seep between the seams of the refurbished pine floorboards, and wasn't about to let the Persian prayer rug she used for a doormat get soiled.

"Where do you want your precious rag that's there now?" he asked.

"The birthing room."

The birthing room was a small space off the kitchen, designed to give 19th-century women privacy during childbirth, while its proximity to the kitchen's open hearth meant boiling water was accessible. The former owners of the sprawling Gothic Revival had used it as a mudroom; Barbara and Lenny had turned it into an office. Although they still referred to it as the birthing room, it had become the catchall for rainy-day carpets, table leaves, mail-order catalogs, and holiday presents.

The house had been built by a prominent banker in the early days of the New Jersey town as a wedding gift for his only daughter and her parson husband. When the daughter died in childbirth, the banker became so crazed that he shot the vicar, drowned the baby, and then committed suicide. A nasty story, Barbara thought, but then these old houses were filled with nasty stories that intrigued her. Rumor had it that the house was haunted; Barbara never doubted it.

The very first night they spent there, Barbara had awakened to the sound of footsteps running up and down the back staircase that led from the birthing room to the second-floor hallway. It had been a child's or woman's pitter-patter, not the heavy tread of a man. A few days later, she had been changing the sheets when the full-length beveled mirror of her bedroom dresser began to violently swing back and forth like a seesaw. Another time, the doorknob rattled and the door shook with the force of someone desperately trying to open it. None of this had frightened Barbara, who believed there were spirits that, for one reason or another, had difficulty moving on to the spirit world. Lenny told Barbara she was just exhausted from the move.

After the birth of the twins, the spirit grew more restless. A force occasionally pushed Barbara as she walked from the kitchen into the birthing room. Sitting at the rolltop oak desk, she often felt a rush of cold air. Assuming that one of the children had come running in from the yard and left the birthing room door ajar, she would check only to find the door tightly shut. When she nursed the twins in the antique armless rocker, an undeniable presence breathed over her shoulder. One hot summer evening, she had pulled down the babies' blankets to the bottom of the crib only to find the babies covered up again later, the blankets tucked neatly under the mattresses.

Convinced that the unhappy spirit of the banker's daughter was behind it all, Barbara enlisted the aid of a tall and straight woman with an excellent reputation for authenticity regarding the extrasensory. The woman wandered through the house and settled in the birthing room, where she felt the spirit's presence most strongly and located the source of its misery. There she meditated, and speaking gently yet with authority, the psychic gave the spirit the permission it had denied itself to leave the house. For a number of years it appeared that the spirit had done just that.

Lately, however, knick-knacks seemed to move from one side of the mantel to the other. Pictures of her children shifted ever so slightly in direction on Victorian lamp tables. From time to time, a red Depression glass vase, always filled with fresh flowers, went from the center of the coffee table to all four of its corners and back again, as though it couldn't decide where it preferred to be.

One day, much to her disappointment—because she had begun to miss the ghost's quirky company—Barbara caught the culprit. It was her mother, very much alive, sneaking out of the living room with a pair of crystal candlesticks and a Limoges candy dish. Norma Ficola stopped in her tracks.

"Don't look so surprised," Barbara told her mother. "You're a dead ringer for the man in the moon who always looks like he got caught with his pants down."

Norma liked new, and she delighted in finally being able to express her decorating preference to her daughter on a daily basis, since she and her husband had relocated from Boston to a new condo development in Barbara's town. Barbara had wanted them to move into an assisted living complex, but Joe Ficola refused to reside with "old people" and swore he'd never set foot in a nursing home. "Better dead," he said of the prospect.

As she confronted Norma with her booty, Barbara understood that her mother would like to smash each fragile item on the floor so she could sweep up the tired past, empty it into the trash, and vacuum up any residue.

"You're lucky to be married to a wealthy man," Norma said. "Why would you want to surround yourself with somebody else's junk?"

***

Yes, Barbara was lucky. Lucky to have been born lucky: the envy of her cousins at every church bazaar and firemen's fair when they were growing up, winning handsome talking dolls, a bicycle, even a deep-fryer. She had slipped into her chosen university with mediocre SATs because the school had been short of women that year. She had never received a speeding ticket or contracted an STD in her youthful days of sexual indiscretion. She had gone on the blind date with a considerably older man who would become her husband because the woman he was supposed to meet that evening had suffered an appendicitis attack. She had been spared widowhood on 9/11 because that husband, who arrived daily at eight a.m. at his brokerage firm in the World Trade Center, had run over someone's mangled muffler and had gotten a flat tire on the George Washington

Bridge. She had conceived twins on the first try—two for the price of one—and enjoyed the financial freedom to stay home and raise them. While she had made the mistake of having a brief affair with her house contractor early on in her marriage, her husband never found out. She was so lucky, she must have stepped in shit, her Uncle Marco used to say. She disliked the expression, because it implied that there was something dirty about her luck—dirty and smelly and hard to get rid of.

"God never gives anyone more than they can handle," Norma liked to say, but Barbara didn't believe that for a second. There were people she knew on whom God just kept dumping problem after problem, as though he was waiting for them to go under, when Lord knows they didn't deserve it. The banker's family had been a perfect example. Thus had Barbara become a prisoner of her own luck, feeling guilty about possessing it but at the same time filled with an overwhelming feeling of responsibility for safeguarding it. Perhaps her good fortune was a result of positive karma—a former life well lived—or the respite before a sorrowful one to come. For Barbara, the past was forever leaking into the present and the present slipping away into the past. This drove her to chronicle everything, from family barbecues and vacations to spelling bees, class plays, and athletic events. Her walls were like museum exhibits; images of ancestors in gilded frames worked their way up her staircase wall and traced her children's lineage on both sides. Vintage typewriters and radios lined a shelf in her family room. One floor-to-ceiling case in the library housed at least 30 leather-bound photo albums in chronological order and rare books with intriguing inscriptions that made

Barbara try to imagine their owners' lives. She saved major newspaper stories, including the sinking of the Titanic, which she had found in the basement of her college dorm.

When she picked up an 18th-century piece of porcelain, it vibrated to her touch, transporting her to its place of origin. She dreamt about dancing with Che Guevara and she could swear she had attended Marie Antoinette's execution. Apart from a genuine desire to preserve history, in some bizarre way she sensed that if she did, her family would continue on a trouble-free path.

"Throw it out!" her husband Lenny insisted. But she couldn't. Not a letter, not an envelope, not Aunt Minnie's dehydrated fox fur with its pointed teeth that Minnie clamped onto its tail to keep it securely draped over her bony shoulders.

When her parents had sold their home in Boston, Barbara cried about all the items her mother had given to the Salvation Army or left out in the street for greedy antiques dealers—complete strangers—to snap up. She hadn't even first offered them to Barbara. Her mother could have jinxed their luck, temped the fates by discarding objects that had held an important place in their lives and in those of countless others—the engineer who had been robbed of his patent, the nonunion assembly-line worker. She never bought something old; but she bought a piece of history, as well as some part of the person who had crafted it. Lenny liked to call her the director of the ASPCJ—the American Society for the Prevention of Cruelty to Junk.

Twice a year, she combed three hundred acres of antiques vendors gathered in a neighboring town with the hopes of coming away with a side table, a piece of carnival glass, even as little as a brass door hinge. It was as though she was bringing home a stray cat left to die a slow death by its owners. She used all this to fill the true gem—the old parsonage she and Lenny had spent years restoring.

She often sat in the living room with a cup of coffee, studying the intricate patterns of the marble hearth or the carved corner moldings around the windows and pretending she was living in an era where she would have been wakened by a servant in a crisp apron and cap. The maid would have arrived with an elegant breakfast on a tray and opened her drapes before preparing her bath. Those were the times when she missed the ghost most, times when she would have liked to pour the banker's daughter a cup of tea or coffee and compare notes. How does it feel for you to be a prisoner? she would have asked. For in their way, they had been kindred spirits—soul mates. Barbara amused herself with the puns; nevertheless, it saddened her to know that she had thrown away her opportunity the one time she had actually disposed of something—or someone—and set the ghost free.

***

Aunt Vita brought her famous rice balls, Aunt Frances her eggplant, Aunt Terry her sesame seed *biscotti*, Aunt Myra her *rugelach*, and Barbara's mother, Norma, store-bought potato salad. The sisters-in-law, all married to Ficola brothers, placed their contributions on the kitchen island and told their daughters to take over.

It had been a slow process for the cousins to "take over" from these women who had commanded so many holiday events, but the older ladies—three Italian, one Jewish, one Yankee—seemed to welcome the chance to retire into the living room where their husbands were already intent on a TV football game before the remainder of the guests arrived.

"I have to stop eating these, Barb," said her skinny cousin Nancy with the short black bob, as she popped another scalding bacon-wrapped scallop into her mouth, and then, taken aback by its temperature, looked for a split second like Olive Oyl if she'd been goosed by Popeye.

"Why? Finally can't fit into your size-four wedding dress?" Barbara said.

"I still can," Nancy protested. "I put it on every anniversary."

"It sneaks up on you," Rosemary said in a bitter tone. This was the first thing she'd uttered since her arrival. "And before you know it, you can't get it off."

The others looked at her, wondering if she was talking about why her husband had left her.

"Could you lower the heat, Barb?" Joanna asked, as with one hand she picked stuffed clams off a baking sheet and arranged them on a platter while her other fanned her face with a dish towel. "I don't know if it's me or the oven."

Now, Joanna, there was a woman who knew that life could pull the rug out and send luck upside on its ass before your very eyes, Barbara thought. What could be worse in this life than the loss of a child? That was even worse than the absence of one for Nancy all those years, until the arrival of little Pierre .

"Want one?" Joanna held the platter in front of Angie, the youngest yet largest woman, with the blond Lady Di hairdo and thick neck who sat quietly folding napkins at the kitchen table. Angie shook her head.

"Nice dress!" Nancy complimented her.

"You can borrow it when you gain a hundred pounds. Better yet, you can hot-water wash it and put it in the dryer, and wear it tomorrow."

Bad genes, bad luck. Poor Angie, Barbara thought; her life was a futile battle to starve herself.

***

Around nine, the lights were dimmed and Barbara carried out a sheet cake ablaze with 61 candles. Lenny inhaled, made a silent wish, and was about to exhale when the candles were snuffed out. The crowd squealed with delight; Lenny pursed his lips and looked at Barbara with admiration. Trick candles. A great stunt to play on a guy who prided himself on being on top of his game. Only Barbara knew there was nothing tricky about the candles. Something warm filled her veins, like a shot of cognac on a cold night: she was back, or more likely she had never gone.

While everyone sat or stood juggling plates, forks, and coffee cups, a group of Lenny's college friends donned leather jackets and sunglasses and performed a rendition of "The Boy from New York City," substituting broker for boy. Matthew and Elena presented a slide show of their father's life assembled from pictures Barbara had given them—ranging from a naked Lenny propped up on a blanket to his most recent golf tournament. The gifts were opened and by ten-thirty it was all over; no one stayed up late anymore. Nancy and Jean-Georges put Pierre to sleep in one guest room; Rosemary retired to the other. Angie's parents went to Norma and Joe's condo. Joanna and Elliott, Angie and her boyfriend Roy, along with other out-of-towners, went to a hotel. Lenny swept back into the dying fire a few burning embers. He flipped off the outside porch light. Barbara vacuumed the kitchen floor.

"The rest can wait until tomorrow," Lenny shouted over the vacuum's roar, beckoning her to follow him upstairs. Barbara's father would never have said that. Even sex didn't trump cleaning up. Joe was never able to rest until every last piece of furniture was in its proper place and every dish had been washed and returned to the cabinet. The Ficolas liked order. And although Barbara was "dead on her feet," as her mother liked to say, from so much work, she stayed up a while longer, until the sink was clear and the living room retained no trace of the festivities.

She had told the twins to make a pass with the vacuum cleaner and to take the gifts to the birthing room, but they had disappeared upstairs without performing either task. They were spoiled, and Barbara knew it had been her own doing. When it came to the house, the children could never meet her standards for perfection, and they had learned to take advantage of their mother's controlling yet good nature. This resulted in Barbara's undertaking everything herself. Barbara made excuses for them, fully aware that she'd been wrong to put so much emphasis on her belongings rather than teaching them responsibility. She picked up the stack of gifts next to the fireplace and carried them into the birthing room.

"It went well, don't you think?" Barbara asked the banker's daughter, as she sank her weary body into the raspberry velvet chaise from another lifetime. The spirit's antics that night had come as no surprise to her. Lately, Barbara had begun to dream that she and Lenny had sold the house. She walked through the echoing rooms that were about to be passed on to new owners just as she had the day they bought the place, and she wept, not under-standing why she was giving up the home she loved—the home where she had raised her children and into which she had poured her identity, the home and belongings she would pass on to generations to come. She'd awake face wet and pillow soaked and, relieved to find herself safely en-sconced in her Cuban mahogany four-poster with its fish-net-fringed canopy, interpret the dream as a directive from the banker's daughter never to sell.

The other day Barbara had misplaced her keys and found them hanging from the outside doorknob of the birthing room. Lenny theorized that a neighbor had spot-ted them in the driveway and put them there, but Barbara believed the spirit had been looking after her.

Before she could fall asleep on the chaise, Barbara forced herself to climb the stairs. She turned the light dim-mer down low for guests who might need to get up during the night—and for the banker's daughter.

***

At one in the morning Barbara heard a distant yet piercing sound. When she realized it was the smoke detector, she jabbed Lenny in the ribs.

"The battery's probably dying," he said, pushing off the covers and shuffling downstairs in his boxer shorts to dis-connect it before it woke the entire house.

"Barb, it's a fire!" he yelled within seconds.

She jumped out of bed and struggled to put on the sweatpants at the foot of the bed, but she couldn't get her legs into the pants. When it dawned on her that she had been fighting with the arms of her sweatshirt, she pulled the shirt over her nightgown and ran to the children's rooms and then the guest rooms, screaming for everyone to get up and out.

Downstairs, Lenny used a fire extinguisher on a small fire in the birthing room to no avail. They were all down now—Matthew and Elena, Rosemary, Nancy, Jean-Georges and Pierre—watching from the kitchen. Matthew filled a pot with water; Barbara called the fire department. It was at this point that the flames caught onto the curtains and the blaze went out of control. Grabbing random outerwear from the hall closet, they all ran out barefoot into the February cold.

Lenny, his bare legs extending beneath his ski jacket, leapt across the lawn and over the shrubbery to the neighbors', where he pounded on the door and rang the bell over and over again until a light went on.

"It's Lenny! My house is on fire!"

***

Barbara had always wondered what she would go for first if she had to suddenly evacuate her home, but as she stood in her neighbors' backyard, watching the firefighters tackle the flames and smoke in the birthing room, she realized that she had taken nothing except the portable kitchen phone she still held in her hand. Dressed in their high boots and long jackets and wide-brimmed hats, dragging hoses across the lawn, carrying hatchets, and shouting unfamiliar terms, the town firefighters entered her home like aliens from another planet. Larry stood beside her with an emasculated expression and slumping shoulders; she knew he felt he had let them down.

"You kept it under control before they got here," she reassured him, but she wished he'd run downstairs faster, or located the fire extinguisher quicker, or done something clever that would have put the damn thing out.

By two-thirty, the birthing room was pretty much gone: what the flames hadn't consumed, the firefighters had destroyed with their chopping. They'd had to smash windows in other parts of the house too, so they wouldn't explode from the heat. The fire had spread into part of the kitchen—her new white kitchen. There was smoke and water damage throughout the house, and water filled the basement; everything would have to be washed, the upholstery steam-cleaned, the cellar carpeting ripped up and thrown out. The firemen told them it was better to sleep elsewhere, so they retrieved their shoes and a few belongings and took up neighbors' offers to house them for the night. They agreed not to inform the rest of the family about the news; morning would be soon enough to upset them.

***

Like restless children forced to nap, Barbara and Lenny lay on the pullout couch in their best friends' home several blocks away. They made a mental list of the calls they would make at the first decent hour: the insurance company, client cancellations, contractors and cleaning services. The firemen thought boxes and torn wrappings left on the birthing room heating grate had caused the fire. Bits of paper and ribbon had fallen through onto the burner of the furnace below.

"But I didn't put the gifts over the grate, Lenny. I'm careful about that. I know I didn't."

"Don't worry. We'll have the house back together for the twins' graduation."

"You don't believe me, do you? You don't believe I didn't put the boxes on the grate."

"Maybe you thought you didn't. You were tired. I only wish you'd come to bed when I asked you. Forget about it now. It could have been a lot worse."

She didn't get a chance to protest further because the phone rang and Lenny was told to pick up. It was the fire department; the entire house was now in flames.

That's how it was with these old houses they said—air in the walls between the laths provided drafts that allowed the smallest hidden embers to take hold. The firefighters couldn't hack into every wall, but they thought they had checked those of the birthing room adequately. By the time a driver of a passing car had called the department on his cell phone, flames were pouring out of the attic windows as well as every other opening.

When Barbara and Lenny neared their block, they found it cordoned off while trucks from six neighboring towns feverishly worked to put out the conflagration. They skipped over hoses that resembled giant boa constrictors, running past the crowd of mesmerized spectators, many in bathrobes, who might have been watching the filming of some big budget movie. The firefighters were hosing down the houses on either side of Barbara and Lenny's in the hope of saving them. Fortunately, the air had been calm

—not the slightest breeze. Water was being directed into the open roof and the windows from hoses connected to cranes on two trucks, one parked in front of the house, the other in the driveway of the house directly behind theirs. The fire raged on.

In her old sweatshirt and nightgown, Barbara stood like a sculpture of a mad bag lady on the lawn across the street, hair sticking every which way, holding a steaming mug of coffee a neighbor had handed her. They had run out of the house as ill-prepared the second time as they had the first.

"It was supposed to rain," Barbara said. "Why doesn't it rain, goddammit, Lenny?"

"Those fuckers are always wrong."

Helpless, she watched the years she had put into documenting, refurbishing, and polishing objects dear to all of them being consumed in an evil paroxysm. This is it, she told herself, this sick feeling in the gut, nothing but darkness and emptiness beyond the present moment; this is how it feels. This is ill fate.

***

The stench of a building fire is different from any other, Barbara thought as they walked around what was left of their home in the daylight. It didn't have the odor of a hearth after a fire has died out, or of the left-over wood that the kids carefully extinguished when they camped. It didn't even stink like a dirty ashtray, though it did stink.

They all stood before a partial shell surrounded by trampled flowerbeds and shrubbery—Barbara and Lenny and the twins, Joe and Norma, Marco and Myra and the rest of the Ficola brothers and wives, Angie and Roy and Rosemary, Nancy and Jean-Georges and Pierre, Joanna and Elliott. The roof was gone, yet the front steps flanked by two stone urns remained intact. The wicker rocker in which Barbara had nursed the twins sat in perfect condition on one side of the property; someone had placed a pot of yellow mums on it. The back staircase still stood, only now it led nowhere. Window sash lay atop scorched piles, framing nothing but splinters of wood, twisted metal, upside-down couches, and appliances thrown on their sides. A floor lamp with a Tiffany shade stuck out of the pile, miraculously unscathed. The trellis door that had led to the plant room behind the birthing room was also intact, except that the plant room now held nothing but burnt bits and pieces. Evidence of their existence, it appeared, had turned into a pile of charred rubble.

The fire chief suggested they demolish what was left of the unstable structure: curious children and thrill-seeking teenagers might get hurt poking around; animals could get trapped inside the debris. So they agreed that the walls of their home would be pushed in and all of it gobbled up by a mechanical Godzilla and spit out into a giant dump truck. Evidence of their existence would be whisked away as easily as Barbara's vacuum cleaner had sucked up any signs of Lenny's birthday festivities.

"I'll get the Tiffany lamp," Lenny said.

"No." Barbara stopped him. "I don't want it."

"You'll build in the spring, sweetheart. A brand-new house," Norma reassured her daughter, seeming excited at the thought.

Tightly clasping the warm hands of her children and with Lenny's arms encircling her from behind, Barbara took in the devastation. She was shocked by her shift of emotions and by the realization that in fact nothing horrific had befallen them. Rather, something very good had occurred. They had survived. Something powerful and catastrophic had taken place, yet they had been spared. Good fortune had prevailed, and Barbara felt an overwhelming sense of being lucky—and liberated.

She tightened her grip on Matthew and Elena, fully aware that no matter what precautions she took, she would always be as susceptible as anyone else to losing those she loved. Flurries spangled the air, and she became aware of the stillness that comes before a good snow. The nursing rocker rocked ever so slightly. Why don't you go? Barbara thought. There's no more house holding you back. You're free too.

Barbara looked down at the white-dusted ground and noticed she was still in her nightgown and sweatshirt and was wearing only one shoe. For the first time since the fire had begun, she was shivering. Before she knew what had happened, she was torn from her children's grasp and on her knees, hands spread to break her fall.

"Barb!" Lenny cried, bending to help her up.

"Careful! Something might be broken," her father warned.

"Oh shit!" her mother said, conceding the ultimate end to a very bad night.

Barbara had not slipped out of her family's hands, nor had she succumbed to stress and fainted. She had most definitely been shoved to the ground. Yet Lenny had been the only one behind her. Now she was certain that she hadn't put the boxes on the grate and that the jealous banker's daughter would never allow herself to be free, no matter how many houses on the property she burned down. The keys on the door, the dreams about moving, Lenny's birthday cake candles, had indeed been a message from her to Barbara—to pack up her intolerable good luck and get going.

St. Mary's Window

Joanna had always possessed the gift. As a child she lay in bed at night and, with the aid of the lamplight shining through her bedroom window in the three-decker in Boston's North End, stared at the picture of Jesus on the wall. It was a peculiar picture her mother had chosen—a print of a blond and blue-eyed hippie-looking Jesus draped in a white robe, seated in an idyllic garden. A boy wearing jacket and tie and short pants sat on Jesus' lap; other youngsters in their Sunday best surrounded him. The blue eyes of the placid Christ peered with delight not at the adoring children but were cast downward at the dressing table that Joanna's mother had decorated with a hand-sewn yellow voile skirt to match the walls. Arranged on top of the table was a supply of bobby pins, curlers, hair spray, pale pink lipstick, cologne and matching scented bath powder: all meant to encourage her daughter's femininity and what her father's family referred to as *la bella figura*, a good image or beautiful appearance.

Each night Joanna, refraining from blinking, concentrated hard on the picture, until Jesus' limp hand rose to bless the children who now animatedly frolicked around the garden, picking daisies and zinnias that swayed in the summer breeze. Her gift was not limited to religious representations: with minimal effort she could turn a wallpaper pattern three-dimensional; she could enter a painting and wander through a building or along forest paths not rendered by the artist.

Yet on this wintry day she could not conjure up the apparition of the Blessed Mother seen on the hospital window by the devout. Insensitive to the frigid temperature, some knelt transfixed, clasped hands supplicating heaven, while others made the sign of the cross or moved their fingers across crystal rosaries, chanting the Hail Mary.

***

She had read about the window in the *Boston Globe*, over her morning bowl of granola and cup of coffee. The faithful were flocking to the delivery entrance of St. Mary's Hospital to pay homage to the image discovered by a man waiting to drive his friend home from a routine colonoscopy.

"Maybe it's because I'm a sinner, because I don't go to church. Maybe that's why God showed her to me," the man was quoted as saying. "Who says it's the Mary? I can come up with several dozen explanations," a bystander claiming to be a high school physics teacher and a lifelong Catholic had argued. "Besides, other apparitions come with a message for people to repent and turn their hearts to God. Where's the message here?" A Harvard psychology professor had reported that such apparitions were classic examples of Gestalt psychology—the mind making sense of a random image. "You are organizing it in a way that is familiar to you, that's meaningful to you," she had said. "It makes sense of that in a familiar way, and a familiar way is faces."

Standing next to Joanna at the site, a short man with an Italian accent and wearing a worn leather jacket and fur-lined hunter's hat outlined to his wife with a gloved finger what he was seeing. In great detail he described a cascading white veil; hands extended outward in an embrace; the shadow of a face. Joanna could make out nothing but a large fogged area that resembled a mountain—narrow at the top, wider at the bottom—nearly covering the entire first-story window.

"It's the Madonna of Guadalupe!" someone shouted from behind.

"Do you know the story of the Guadalupe?" a Hispanic woman on the other side of Joanna whispered to her. The woman wore a leopard-patterned chiffon kerchief knotted beneath her chin and a brown quilted parka. Middle-aged, she was probably not much older than Joanna, with a serene but lined face that invited speculation about what had given this woman joy in life and what had caused her despair. Joanna's mother would have approved of her perfectly applied makeup. This woman in her elegant kerchief would never run out of the house as Joanna sometimes did, looking slovenly and hoping not to bump into someone she knew. The spiciness of her perfume reminded Joanna of benediction after High Mass.

"Not really," Joanna admitted. She knew little about the legend, except that back in the 80s she and her husband, Elliott, had seen the image hanging in every dusty bar and bus stop in Mexico.

"A very long time ago Our Lady of Guadalupe appeared to a peasant in the countryside near what is now Mexico City. She asked him to have a church built in her honor, to prove the people's love. When the peasant told the bishop, the bishop asked for a sign of proof of this story. He sent the peasant to a place where roses couldn't possibly grow, yet he found them there nevertheless. He filled his *tilma* (the woman described with her hands a blanket worn over the man's front and back) with them. When he emptied the *tilma* of roses in front of the bishop, they saw that the Virgin had left her image on it. The *tilma* and the image still exist today."

A man in front of Joanna turned and corrected the woman: "I believe it's Our Lady of Fatima." He was tall and distinguished-looking, with glistening hair combed straight back; in his trench coat he could be a Burberry ad in the *New York Times*. The confidence he exuded reminded Joanna of Elliott.

The Italian man disagreed, said it was the Madonna of Mount Carmel. Every Little Italy in America had a church and school and social club named after her, Joanna thought. "But then where's the infant Jesus?" the Italian man's wife asked.

As an artist, Joanna knew about the illusions light and shadows could cause. Still, her trained eyes could see nothing that resembled the detailed descriptions being offered. According to that newspaper psychologist, shouldn't her brain have been organizing the information she'd been gathering about the image to produce a familiar shape when she looked at the window?

"I see it!" A young woman called out to Joanna's frustration. "I'm praying and I'm seeing it."

Joanna no longer prayed. She had rejected the tenets of Catholicism in her 20s. She had prayed to God when her daughter Jill's life was on the line, but her prayers had been ignored.

She stayed there for about half an hour, more intent on the onlookers than on the supposed apparition. Mothers held gold and silver medals bearing the Virgin's image next to children in wheelchairs. A cluster of women, most likely nuns, given their clean-scrubbed faces and angelic voices, sang: "Ave Maria our hearts are on fire ... Ave, Ave, Ave Maria." People took pictures with their phones. Joanna preferred to use a 35 millimeter camera, but she had forgotten to bring it—left it on the kitchen counter, along with her cell.

"Do you see it? It's a miracle," someone said.

***

The Virgin Mary sure as hell was no stranger to Joanna. Her mother had always maintained a special devotion to the saintly woman who was also a Jewish convert and mother of an only child and with whom Joanna's mother must have identified. Even her mother's name, Myra, was a derivative of Mary—and probably Mary was a derivative of the Hebrew Myra. A foot-tall statue of Mary in the image of the Immaculate Conception sat on her mother's bureau.

It was in that likeness that Joanna's mother had dressed Joanna one Halloween, putting a white cotton bathrobe on her backwards in an exact replica of the gown the statue wore. Next she sewed gold trim on a piece of blue silky fabric and draped it around Joanna's head and shoulders. Seven-year-old Joanna had been the laughingstock of the neighborhood when she knocked on doors and when asked who she represented answered: "The Blessed Virgin Mary." "That's-a so nice," the little Italian grandmothers said, pinching her cheek, while the parents of Joanna's friends could hardly contain themselves.

***

Home from the hospital site, Joanna searched online for those familiar images of her mother's patron saint and printed them out along with their legends. First was Our Lady of Guadalupe: Mary, hands together in prayer, wore a full-length greenish cape that covered her head and shoulders and a pinkish gown dotted with gold; she was bathed in a golden aura. Next she found Our Lady of Fatima, who repeatedly appeared to three children in Portugal to preach about the necessity for peace after the First World War. Joanna printed out the picture of Mary clad in a dress not unlike the one she had donned that infamous Halloween, but it was a white—not blue—cape edged in gold that this Mary wore. Joanna agreed with the Italian man's wife that the apparition couldn't be the Madonna of Mount Carmel since her pointed crown—like the one on the statue she remembered seeing paraded through the North End of Boston during Italian feasts—did not fit the rounded edges of the one on the mountainous smudge. She typed in "Our Lady of Lourdes", who appeared 18 times to the poor 14-year-old French girl Bernadette and asked her to have a chapel built on the spot. Her solid white gown with a blue sash was a possibility.

Joanna took the printouts up to her studio. Ever since Jill's death, she'd become a visitor there, a tourist trying to imagine the life of a talented artist who had abandoned the space. Joanna breathed in the scent of oil paint, but her fingertips no longer tingled with possibilities. She removed the canvas she was currently working on from her easel: a scene of the villa she and Elliott had stayed at on their last trip to Italy, a sprawling stone edifice amid a backdrop of hills—the place where she had found little Elisabetta, whom she believed to be the reincarnation of her daughter. She was working from a photo Elliott had taken on an early morning walk their first day there, but the image in lugubrious brownish green tones could be taken for twilight or dawn—the most ambiguous times of day, when even the sky is ambivalent about its intentions and the improbable becomes possible.

Her earlier work had depicted surreal landscapes with people flying over water and birds plowing fields. But it was the psychological situation that she came to find more surreal: the tenuous balance of the conscious and the unconscious, between people's dreaming and waking states.

The villa was the first painting she'd attempted since the accident, and she refused to place figures in it. A life-sized painting of a 12-year-old Jill seated on a stairwell reading a book graced a wall of the newly renovated middle school. In bold colors—blacks, greens, and reds—Joanna had captured the internal struggle between childhood and adolescence, and now it hung as a memorial to her daughter. Unbeknown to anyone except Elliott, Joanna had begun a portrait of her father, using a photo Elliott had taken of him at a Red Sox game at Fenway Park. But her distinct psychological acumen had failed her. What stared back at her was a stiff, embalmed visage from which she recoiled. No, she would not portray people to whom she could not give a soul.

Today she used pastels in order to work faster, and fleshing out the texture and folds of the fabrics, the composition and gleam of the gold threads. Oddly enough, everything ended up in the same greenish brown hues that suggested an impending storm.

***

"How long have you been working on these?" Elliott asked when he found her in the studio. Four large pictures hung on a clothesline stretched across the white walls of the room.

"All day."

"What are they?"

"Different images of the Virgin Mary. Can't you tell?"

"I'm an atheist, remember?"

"They're horrible."

"No."

"Don't indulge me, Elliott. It makes me feel like I'm killing time in a therapeutic craft center for the insane."

"Fine. Did you get a commission from the Pope?"

"I just couldn't stop."

"She had quite a wardrobe. Wonder who her tailor was."

"In the church I went to as a kid, she even wore jewelry," Joanna informed him.

"Carpentry must have been lucrative in those days."

"You're really bad, you know."

"I'm so bad I think I'll eat the green one of your pictures for dinner."

"Sorry. I lost track of time."

"I can grab a bite on my way to the hospital."

She wanted to make him something. He'd kept his promise to stop stuffing himself with junk as a means of dealing with his grief, and he was back to his trim self, maybe even better.

"Do you feel like breakfast or dinner?" she asked.

"I guess I wouldn't mind something substantial. The five-minute sandwich break in the ER storage room is getting old."

"Got time for something out of the freezer?" She turned off the studio lights; she had worked nonstop into darkness.

"What should I take out, Jo?"

"I'll get it. You'll never find anything in there. Frankly, I don't even know what I've got."

"Didn't you forget something in those pictures?" he asked on their way downstairs.

"What do you mean?"

"None of them have faces."

In the kitchen she ran a Tupperware container of tomato vegetable soup under hot water, plopped the red chunk of ice into a saucepan, and set it on the stove.

"This still good?" Elliott was pointing to a small baking dish of leftover moussaka in the refrigerator.

"Take off the aluminum foil first and cover it with a paper towel," she reminded him. "Why didn't you tell me about the window?" She placed clumps of grated cheddar in two bowls for the hot soup to melt.

"Oh, now I get it. I didn't even hear about it until this morning, and not much at that. It's not in my hospital, and even if it was, in my line of work bashed-in skulls take precedence over dirty windows."

Elliott's lack of interest irritated her. People's perceptions, particularly visual ones, fascinated her. The spirit world fascinated her. Neither titillated Elliott, who still refused even to consider that Elisabetta might be Jill.

"The crowd was really something, Elliott."

"You went to see it? Today? While I was sleeping?"

"Why are you surprised? Life goes on when you snooze. They're calling it a miracle."

He laughed and set down two plates on the island in front of two stools. "You know what a miracle is? When the battery that lights up the blade on my laryngoscope doesn't die while I'm going down someone's throat, or when I enter a code blue on the floor and all the equipment I need is there and the room isn't in utter chaos. Mineral deposits in water that gets inside a broken seal between two windows is not a miracle in my book."

"But is what they see a miracle?" she asked. "I remember learning in catechism class that a miracle was an act of faith."

"It's wishful thinking—imagination."

"I have a good imagination, and I couldn't see it. I wanted to see what they saw."

"Then you have to believe what they believe."

"Will you go there with me?"

"Joanna, I'm heading out to my third consecutive 12-hour shift."

"When you get off."

"That's not fair. I don't really care about this window. You do. You have all day to go back."

"But I'd like you to come with me. I've lost my skill, Elliott. The sun in my paintings is cold; the wind doesn't blow. Or maybe that's my interpretation. Death. Death to everything! That's what I see. You said you wanted me to let you in, so I'm asking you to do something important with me. I'm letting you in, and you're fucking refusing. You have your ER to go to for redemption. You couldn't save Jill, but you get a chance to make up for it every day. What about me, Elliott? What do I do? Where do I go?"

Joanna threw the spoon she was using to stir the defrosting soup onto the stove; it fell with a clang onto the tile floor and bounced around, splattering red droplets in every direction as she stomped out of the kitchen. She walked upstairs. She fell onto her bed, and she cried. He didn't follow her. His guardrails were up, caution lights ablaze. She knew she'd hit him hard where he hurt the most. Their fear of one another was the price they now paid for having suffered the painful consequences of unconditional parental love.

When he had left for work, she went to the attic, cluttered with bags of old appliances and boxes of dishes and glasses and silverware she had been saving for Jill's first apartment. Unable to navigate the crammed space with its low slanted ceiling, she threw her body onto the bags and boxes and began to swim over what her father would call crap—rolled-up rugs and cartons of books, old curtains, space heaters, lamps—until she came upon a carton labeled in blue ink in her mother's handwriting: "Joanna's desk."

She knew it was there, under a basket of two fake furry kittens into whose stuffed bodies Joanna (the creative child, as everyone called her) had once breathed so much life that they seemed to purr. It was there in the pink plastic box with the tarnished brass clasp and the image of a teenager with a long black ponytail on the lid. Holding the box, she executed a reverse breaststroke with her free arm until she landed on the wide pine planks of the attic. She sat on the floor and rummaged through the box, finding letters her cousins had sent about boyfriends and unfair parents, and a note from a boy in high school who told her she was the meanest girl he'd known because she'd rebuffed him in the middle of the school cafeteria. She had hated him for that note, but now she felt sorry that she'd been so cavalier about his feelings—a bitch, really. She picked up a hard-as-a- rock piece of penny candy a boy she had once had a crush on in fifth grade had sent sailing across the classroom onto her desk. There were postcards she had mailed home from her summer abroad in Spain at the end of her junior year. Her penmanship had been impeccable; even that had deteriorated, to the point where now she could hardly read her own script.

Then she found it near the bottom: a piece of white paper with a purple map of the Middle East. It bore no city or country names or labels of any kind, just masses of purple splattered with translucent grease stains. It had hung on her aunt Norma's refrigerator door for years, and one day Joanna had stolen it, never admitting the theft when her family had decided it had fallen off the refrigerator door, been mistaken for trash, and thrown away.

If you stared at the map long enough, you saw the face of Christ. A few people had taken only minutes, others hours or even days, to decipher the image. Some never saw it. Joanna had detected it within seconds. Whenever she looked at the picture after that, all she could see was Christ's face. She held up the jagged blob of purple, taped it on the wall, and stood back a few feet. She closed one eye, then the other. She stared until her eyes crossed and blurred. Nothing. Her artistic vision—her ability to make lips suggest a smile, eyes threaten to blink and tear, veins pulsate and skin radiate warmth—had been blinded. Perhaps it had been a mistake to think that, because her mind took her beyond the obvious, she deserved to bring those mysteries back to this world.

* * *

She went to bed wishing she had contracted the wicked bad cold from the man who sat next to her on the T the other day on her way home from Macy's winter clearance sale. She longed for a good flu, a fever that would not only garner sympathy but also excuse her from all obligations for a week or two—such as talking to Elliott. She was sinking farther into the place to which she had traveled after Jill died.

She got up and checked her e-mail, then her voice mail. Maybe she'd missed a message from Nancy or Barbara while she was swimming in the attic. But it wasn't only from her cousins or friends she needed to hear. Elliott alone bore witness to the burden of her craft—to her sixth sense, her third eye. Elliott alone shared Jill's absence in the quiet of the night while they lay side by side, barely breathing.

She returned to the studio and studied the facial features in the printouts she'd taped to the corners of her pastels. The generic button nose in every image was so unlike her mother's prominent yet attractive Sephardic version. The eyes were lackluster, and the parted rosebud lips wanton for someone who should have been grinning from ear to ear to have a son who turned out to be God. But these artists hadn't seen the Virgin, so what had given them the right to depict a woman who looked spaced out in orgasmic ecstasy or on a heroin high? She went back to bed.

***

"Take the T in and meet me here at the ER in an hour," Elliott said on the phone, waking her at six the following morning. "We'll drive over to St. Mary's. Gotta run,"

She didn't ask why he had changed his mind. Thoughts of cutting up his favorite shirt, never cooking him another meal, or telling his mother on him evaporated. On the 11 o'clock news the night before, an interview with St. Mary's senior vice-president of marketing had revealed that the window would be dismantled in two days. Detailed inspection by glass experts had determined that a vacuum seal had broken, allowing water to seep between the panes, which was nothing unusual. What was unusual, however, said the bishop of the archdiocese of Boston, was the well-defined outline the seepage pattern had produced.

"The church is very, very cautious in situations like this," he said. "The window will be examined for perhaps years before a decision about its validity can be determined."

"Regardless of whether or not the image is that of the Virgin," the hospital's spokesperson confirmed, "it must be removed. It's hampering the functioning of the hospital, even though the crowds have been quite orderly."

***

The parking garage was full. Elliott found a spot several long blocks away; as they carefully trudged over uneven, icy sidewalks, Joanna waited for him to regret his decision to accompany her.

At St. Mary's, more onlookers than had been there the day before jammed the delivery entrance and lined both sides of the street. Bouquets and hundreds of candles had turned a dumpster below the window into an altar, with more bouquets several feet deep around it. Hospital security guards tried to keep the crowd from spilling into the street, while police directed traffic. Joanna and Elliott made their way through the murmuring worshippers to get a better view.

"Well?" Joanna asked. The sun was brighter than yesterday, bringing more color on the pane.

"Honestly, if I tell myself it's an impressionistic image of the ones you showed me of her, I guess I could convince myself that that's what I'm seeing, especially given the fact that I'm exhausted and headed to dreamland. But since I don't believe in those images in the first place, what I see is something that could look like anything from Mount Washington to a pile of mashed potatoes."

"Then I should also be able to see her if I tell myself that's what it is, but I still can't. What the hell is wrong with me, Elliott? I don't even see the outline of the veil everyone talks about."

A woman inclined her head toward Joanna and spoke softly. "You can argue about what is in the window, but *señora*, there is no arguing about the faith of the people who are gathered here because of their love for her."

Joanna recognized the voice and scent of the woman with the leopard kerchief who had spoken to her about the Guadalupe the day before. She turned, amazed that they had managed to land beside each other again, but the woman had moved on as quickly as she had arrived.

"Had enough?" Elliott asked.

Joanna was about to accede when a man climbed onto the dumpster, crushing flowers and knocking over candles.

He was in his 20s or early 30s, of average height, with a red beard and shoulder-length dreadlocks. His hair matched the fiery sky on his sleeveless sweatshirt, which left his muscular arms exposed to the freezing cold. The crowd gasped, then fell silent.

"They're going to take the window tomorrow morning. Are we going to stand for that?" the man shouted. "This is our Blessed Mother. They should build a chapel so more people can come. Are we going to let them take her away?"

"No!" a voice called out, followed by another and yet another, until the no's reverberated through the crowd.

"Over my dead body!" cried the young man, his arms outstretched as if to guard the window.

"Build a shrine! Build a shrine!" the crowd began to chant.

"It's Jesus! Look! He's Jesus!" someone yelled.

"I think it's time to ask for the check," Elliott said.

"Get down!" someone called out to the man. "Go home!" more voices cried.

Two security guards, one black and one white, set out for the man. Trampling the makeshift shrine, they climbed onto the dumpster.

"Go home!" half the crowd was yelling. "Build a shrine!" the other half screamed.

An unopened can of Coke sailed above Joanna and Elliott's heads, missing the guards and the man, and hitting the window. It left a hole in the upper left corner.

"Let's get the hell out of here." Elliott took Joanna's hand and pulled her through the deafening crowd. Rosary beads clutched to their breasts, women were crying while men cursed either the police or the young man. A stream of cruisers arrived, sirens blaring, lights flashing.

"Holy shit!" Elliott said when they were settled into their car.

"Holy shit!" Joanna repeated.

***

They breakfasted at a little Cuban restaurant on the corner of Centre and Paul Gore Streets in Jamaica Plain. He ate a roast pork sandwich with side orders of black beans, rice, and ripe plantains, along with a tall glass of fresh orange juice. All she could manage were two eggs over easy and whole-wheat toast.

She liked the way the simplicity of the décor set off the artwork on the walls, the bold but simple lines and vibrant palette of Caribbean artists.

"Thanks for coming with me." She sipped thick hot chocolate from an oversized black mug with a cinnamon stick in it.

He reached across the lacquered wooden table and covered her hand with his. "Wouldn't have missed it," he said, his tired eyes taking her in—drawing her in, asking if the morning had been disappointing, empowering her with his love. She would stay with him always.

***

Forty-five minutes later, lying on their king-sized bed in nothing but his shorts, he clicked his teeth several times, a signal that he had entered the first stage of sleep. Fully clothed, she climbed in beside him and rested her head on the nest of his hairy chest as it rhythmically rose and fell. There she remained staring sideways at the painting she had purchased from a gallery in Rockport, that hung on the opposite wall, until the man in a tuxedo and the lady in a long purple gown began to sway to the notes the musician beside them coaxed out of the trumpet he caressed. Round and round they twirled, sinking their feet into the wet sand. The tide repeatedly kissed the shoreline goodbye and pulled farther and farther away. It grew chilly as the orange sun dipped ever so slowly below the horizon, where the woman with the leopard kerchief and perfectly applied makeup smiled at Joanna, lifted a brown-sleeved arm, and stroked across the bay.

Pretty Face

"I hope you're not doing this for me," Roy said. "I like you just the way you are. You've never been fat in my eyes."

"Then you're blind," Angie fired back.

She had made it perfectly clear on their first date that she was seriously considering having vertical gastric bypass surgery. She hadn't said it to impress him, but rather to warn him of her intentions. Risks or no risks, whether or not Roy liked her fat, she'd made one of the most important decisions of her life, and for once she had no doubt that it was the right one. This was about her. Besides, did he really find her attractive below the double chin?

"I saw that face, when you pulled into the parking lot of the Branding Barn, and I shouted, 'Hee haw!' I got so excited," he had said when she answered his personal ad in the local newspaper. "I didn't even see your body."

But that was just it: he hadn't looked at her body, and nothing about her body had made him want to look.

She knew she had a pretty face; she had been told that her whole life. It was amazing how people always categorized her anatomical parts when it came to compliments. She also had a pretty smile and pretty hair. Her ears were referred to as perfectly formed and petite. It was as though people were scrambling to name anything they could above the neck, because the neck and all the rest was too broad to take in, too grotesque to view. Once in junior high school, without her knowing, a boy had taped onto the back of her T-shirt a sign that read OVERSIZE LOAD, in red Magic Marker. He then attempted to wave the hallway traffic out of her way. When she caught on, she'd laughed, then locked herself in a stall in the girls' bathroom and cried for the entire period she should have been in chorus. Oh yes—she had a lovely voice.

However, she'd been a heroine in her family as a small child, unlike her cousin Nancy, who'd been made to suffer alone at the table so long after dinner that the greasy juice surrounding her steak hardened into white wax. Angie couldn't comprehend Nancy's lack of appetite. At family gatherings, Angie had been the first of the cousins—even faster than some adults—to clean her plate. The other children peeled off the hated chicken skin and sneaked it to Angie. They slipped her the burnt pieces of roasted potatoes. They fought to sit next to her, in easy shot of her dish. No one wanted to be ostracized and made to suffer like Nancy, whose mother once forced her to dunk a Genoa salami sandwich into a glass of chocolate milk, promising that it would be more palatable that way. No, they had Angie to thank for their after-dinner freedom. And Angie had her expandable stomach to thank for her popularity. Why couldn't Nancy be more like Angie? the adults asked as they monitored Nancy's mouthfuls and Angie took the seconds and thirds that were offered her. She accepted the chicken skins and the leftover sausage links, she lifted two éclairs off of a platter of pastries, she ate tripe and stuffed rolled pigskin simmered in tomato sauce when her cousins wouldn't touch the stuff. She ate and ate. And the more she ate, the more she was held up as an example for the others to emulate. While Nancy's parents fretted over their malnourished daughter, who was all legs and arms, and forced her to drink tonics to stimulate her appetite, Angie's mother and father preened at having produced such a healthy offspring.

Then puberty made its debut, and before Angie knew what had happened, everything seemed to change. By the time they were 15, Nancy's angles had smoothed out into subtly proportioned curves. Even her appetite had improved. Angie, however, remained one enormous measurement, from below her thick neck to her buttocks. Her thighs rubbed together when she walked. Her feet burst the straps of her shoes. Now the negative attention was cast onto Angie. She was too heavy, they all warned her parents. It wasn't healthy; it wasn't nice for a young girl. They must do something before she burst.

"Nonsense, it's all muscle," Doctor Mazzo, her pediatrician, had said.

After all, she'd won a swimming tournament at the Y in sixth grade—the first girl, the youngest girl in the family, to take part in athletics.

"And," he had added (he was privy to gossip about his patients), "I hear she has a boyfriend. What are you worried about?" She needed the nourishment, he insisted; the exercise and the desire to be loved would keep her weight in check.

Love did sustain Angie, until she was a size 16 and her boyfriend threatened that, if she gained another pound, he was gone. When she tipped the scales at 210, he called her a cow and broke up with her. Her parents' eyelids flew up like window shades.

"I'll buy you a fur coat if you lose 25 pounds," her father, Sal, offered.

"I'll take you to Italy," her mother, Terry, said.

"You'll be able to fit in an airplane seat," Sal added.

But there had been no comforting words for Angie, only comforting food—lots of it—sneaked into her room after her parents retired for the evening, bought from vending machines at her community college, shared with cousins who pretended that her eating habits were normal, that everything about her was normal, because they loved her. As Dr. Mazzo had said, love was sustaining.

***

Angie filled out the questionnaire from the Bayside Surgical Group that arrived in the mail. List every diet you've ever been on and the results. Where should she begin? Nancy had announced her engagement just around the time fen-phen had come on the market. Lose weight; eat like a normal person, the ad had said. It was supposed to be taken for only two months; Angie took it for three. She lost 50 pounds and she developed a leaky heart valve. At least she hadn't died, like some others who had taken the drug, although there were times when she wished she had.

She had refused the fur coat and the trip to Italy. Despite the weight loss, her mother had had to sew her bridesmaid's dress while her cousins bought theirs off the rack. In every one of Nancy's wedding pictures, she hid behind the other attendants and in her cousin Rosemary's wedding photos, and in Barbara's and Joanna's. Nancy's wedding had bothered her most, however; maybe because Nancy and she were only two days apart in age. She had seen countless black-and-white photos of them wrapped in bunting and held up for the camera by their mothers on their first day home from St. Mary's hospital as though to say: Look what we've just done! Nancy and she had grown up like Siamese twins, side by side in identical attached row houses. They had held hands in line on their first day of kindergarten, eaten lunch in school cafeterias together, and later hung out at bars together. They had never been served at the same time, however. When Angie put her empty glass down, it remained empty, but Nancy's no sooner hit the counter than bartenders would appear with a refill.

"You know, I've been looking at you for 15 minutes," Angie once chewed out a male server. "As soon as my cousin takes her last sip, you're there. Why is that? Because she's thin and I'm not?"

"I didn't see you," the young bartender had stammered.

"Bullshit!"

But he had been right on the mark. Her bulk made her invisible.

After the fen-phen near fatality, she had tried Meridian, then Dexatrim. She added them to the list. Then Weight Watchers, Jenny Craig, the Stillman water diet, the Atkins fat diet, the South Beach diet, the ice cream diet, the Hollywood miracle juice diet. She had done them all—countless times. She had lost a little but gained it all back and more. For six months she had drunk nothing but Slimfast, then gagged on a piece of steak and had to have her cousin Joanna's doctor-husband perform the Heimlich on her at a family barbecue. NutriSystem products made her vomit. NuSkin

Appeal shakes gave her gas. Chocolate-and-vanilla flavored Ayds appetite suppressants had added 15 pounds and made her a size 24.

Are there any eating disorders in the family? Yes, if she counted her own compulsion. She had tried purging once, but it disgusted her. She circled no. Then came the list of risks: one in every 200 died from the surgery. Angie put the pen down.

"You don't have to do this," Roy sang out, his chin resting on the crown of her head. She felt the vibration of his jaw.

"At work today one of the residents asked if I'd gained weight. God bless old people; what's on their minds is on their tongues."

"You're around too many old people."

"I work in a nursing home."

"Get a new job."

"I love my work. Besides, it isn't easy for me to get hired. I can't bear to look at one more personnel officer's condescending stare and hear them tell me how the job has just been filled."

"You're exaggerating."

"I live this, Roy, you don't. Do you know that sometimes I have to move furniture around in the rooms to get closer to patients? Wheelchairs fit better in most spaces than I do!"

"Let's go to bed."

"That's your answer to everything. You don't have to make me feel better all the time."

"Honey." He only called her that, the pitch of his voice rising as he pronounced the word, when he wanted to point out that he was right and she was wrong. "You think I only make love to you for your sake?"

Angie always took a long time to get ready to retire. She liked Roy to be in bed when she arrived so she could shut off the lights before she slipped in alongside him.

"Keep it on," Roy said, indicating the light.

But she doused it just the same, and unbuttoned the gaily printed smock of her uniform and unhooked her bra, releasing the heavy weight of her breasts. She felt their warmth against the cool skin that protected her heart. She tugged down the elastic waistband of her white polyester trousers, taking the panties down along with them. She had forgotten what it was like to unfasten zippers and buttons. She couldn't imagine life as the light-as-a feather woman a man whisked into his arms and spun around and wouldn't put down because he wanted her with him wherever he went.

"Ta-da!" she exclaimed when the last article of clothing was off. Then she lifted the covers and performed her vanishing act before Roy's pupils had time to adjust to the blackness and he saw her body, covered with the white quilt, looking like Mont Blanc. He kissed her lips and face. He sucked on her nipples. He fondled her clitoris. And he entered her. Spot A. Spot B. Spot C. Spot D. He might have been on a road trip, hitting brief but familiar rest stops until reaching his final destination. For Angie, this was making love. She was grateful for the attention and felt she didn't deserve to ask him to linger here and there a while longer.

***

Angie's parents liked Roy. He wasn't a lawyer or a doctor or a high-powered stockbroker, but he was solid, hardworking, and devoted to their 42-year-old daughter. He also, most likely, represented her last chance for babies. It was more for Angie, though, that they hoped for grandchildren: how could anyone—especially a woman—live without children, without a family? No one had ever believed that childless Nancy and Jean-Georges were really happy—not until little Pierre, that is, came along. Childlessness had been the one negative trait Angie and Nancy shared, but then Pierre materialized out of nowhere to remove the last shred of solidarity. Despondent and jealous, Angie had agreed to a blind date with a friend of a friend whom nobody knew very well. He waited for Angie in the parking lot of a popular local bar, just as Roy would one day do. But when he saw Angie get out of her car and walk toward the entrance, he stopped her and suggested they might prefer a quieter, more intimate place in the next town. They could talk more easily and get to know each other better; he would follow her there in his car. When Angie pulled out of the parking lot and took a left in the direction of the designated restaurant, he took a right. She left unreturned messages on his voice mail, then shut herself in her room for days, until her parents had to break down the door because she had fainted from dehydration.

***

Her appointed nutritionist found Angie's body mass index acceptable for the procedure. The psychotherapist confirmed that she did not have an eating disorder. Fine with me, Angie told herself, thinking that if she wasn't a walking eating dysfunction, who was? Her required attendance at support group meetings was to be spread out over a six-month period and, while one meeting a month would have sufficed, Angie attended more frequently to prove how much she wanted the surgery. She listened as lecturers identified themselves as if they were addressing an AA group and explained in painful detail how they had become obese and what had led them to surgery. All were now average weight—normal looking. Their lives had changed.

About a week before Angie's surgery, she began to experience pain radiating from below her breastbone when she got up to pee during the night. She attributed it to stress and, breaking the rules, told no one, knowing that if she did, the surgery would be postponed for who knew how much longer.

"If I die," she said to Roy the night before her big day, "make sure you pick up all your clothing off the floor and hide it. My parents still don't know we live together. They can't believe you'd want to."

It was a joke. Getting in the first laugh about herself had become a habit, one that made it less likely that someone else would laugh at her. It was the fat person's secret to jolliness, yet Roy had never found it funny.

"We could have gotten married a long time ago," he said.

Several hours later she was still unable to sleep, running her hand over the smooth flesh of her stomach for the last time before it was cut open and left to scar. She woke Roy up. "What time is it?"

"Two a.m."

"Four and a half more hours until we leave for the hospital?" she said with a sigh.

"You really ought to try and get some sleep. Tomorrow's a big day."

"I think I'm losing my nerve."

"You've just got cold feet. Before you know it, it'll all be over." He put his arm around her and pulled her closer. "But remember, you can always change your mind, because as much as I'll try to help, this is something you have to do alone, Ange. You're in this by yourself. "

***

A four-hour surgery turned into eight due to an ugly gray gallbladder—the source of her prior discomfort—that was hard to cut through. And so it took additional time to trim away the top part of her stomach and block the bottom, to make a new sac the size of an egg, to take part of her intestine and bypass it to the new stomach, which would allow food to pass through her faster, without sufficient time for digestion. After three days she was sent home with a diet of puréed foods. On her post-op visit, the nutritionist told her to eat the way she wanted, that she would know when she was full. She tried but, by the time she felt full, she had already become too full, and was nauseated.

Certain foods made her gums and mouth tingle. She became lightheaded, and crawled around the kitchen floor tiles in search of the coolest spot, like a dog lying down on a hot summer day. Roy placed cold compresses on her forehead while water seeped out of her pores and onto the floor. Her sweatpants became soaked until they could absorb no more. Unable to move, she watched until she was sitting in a puddle of her own body fluids. Why was she still wearing sweatpants? She was supposed to be thin now. She was supposed to be normal.

"Get me out of my clothes," she implored Roy. "Get me out of my clothes! I'm drowning!"

They promised it would get better: the doctor, the nutritionist, the former patients at the support lectures all promised her, and it did. She learned how to adjust to this new digestive system of hers that had been turned upside down, right side up, and inside out. They told her to eat her proteins first, then her vegetables, then her carbohydrates, but when she did, it made her sick. She changed the order, but had to constantly juggle it. No sooner had she found foods that agreed with her, than they turned on her, just as men had. Peanut butter gave way to ham, which gave way to hard-boiled eggs, which led to cheese. Sweets lowered her blood sugar. Caffeine and pasta put her to sleep. She slept for days—weeks—shivering under two heavy quilts.

On her first day back at work, she missed her stop getting off the bus. She hadn't seen it coming, and before she knew it, they were past it. But when had it become the last stop on the route? She ran frantically up and down the aisle as unfamiliar landmarks whizzed by, but she could not bring herself to ask to be let off. The bus driver ignored her. She sat back down, immobilized by frustration all the way to the terminal, where she waited for what seemed like an eternity until the driver began his return route.

"Too late," they said when she arrived at the nursing home.

"But I'm here," she insisted, going for a wheelchair to take Mrs. Dunphy for her morning stroll.

"Too late, too late," they chanted—staff and residents alike. "You've been gone too long. You are too late."

She became Mrs. Roy Ostrander. She lost 50 pounds in six months, 120 in a year. She went from a size 26 to a 10, just the way they had said she would. The sight of her in any reflective surface never failed to take her by surprise.

She felt so much lighter. She went back to the nursing home to beg for her old job. When they didn't recognize her, she pretended to be a new applicant and was hired on the spot. She was amazed at being able to slide in between night-stands and beds, with room to spare. She floated through the closing doors of the crowded elevator in the lobby. No opening seemed too small for her to pass through; she was like a mouse, a phantom.

"Why so glum?" the director asked one morning. She smiled less now than before; there was no need to be jolly anymore; people noticed and liked her despite her mood. They all saw her now, especially Roy, who studied every blemish, every mosquito bite, every black-and-blue.

"Shouldn't you wear something over that?" he asked as they left for dinner one evening.

"Why?"

"You'll be cold."

And she was cold. She was always cold, so cold a thin layer of ice formed on her skin, like frost on a windowpane.

"Don't worry. Expect the abnormal," Dr. Barter said. "Your body is no longer normal. Nothing about you is or-dinary now."

"But ice, Dr. Barter?"

"Not to worry."

Angie dropped pounds without trying. She didn't bother to weigh herself anymore. Ashamed to take her clothes to the tailor after they'd been altered several times, she bought new outfits instead. This weight-loss thing was costing her a fortune.

"Ange, I'm afraid you might be taking this too far. You're downright skinny," Nancy said on Christmas Eve, as they set the table at Nancy's house. Angie now was, in fact, the same size as Nancy.

"You're not jealous, are you?"

"Look, Angie, I've been like this my entire life. But you haven't."

That night Nancy caught Angie and Jean-Georges in the sandbox behind her house. Angie hadn't been able to help herself; she'd always been attracted to Jean-Georges. She had come on to him because he was so handsome in the blue polo shirt that accentuated those turquoise eyes of his. His was trim where Roy was pudgy, and he was French, which went a long way. Her groin ached when she looked at him across the dining room table. She hadn't known if he would follow her out, but then he was there beside her. They sat down in the sandbox and kissed, with the full moon highlighting their entwined bodies. She could have kissed him forever. She took his hand and pressed it hard between her legs and convulsed with painful satisfaction. What she had done—all of it— was fine, just the normal abnormal behavior Dr. Barter had warned her about. Danny Haynes had pulled her pants down in the sandbox in his yard when they were eight, only it had been summer then, and she had been mortified. Angie's sole concern about her encounter with Jean-Georges had been the awful cold she felt out there on the hard frozen sand with her skin exposed to snow that fell and stung her belly.

By the time Easter rolled around, Angie was thinner than Nancy. She had started wearing baggy clothes again to hide the skeletal frame that drew stares as if she were a freak in a sideshow. Her parents didn't need to worry about her nourishing a fetus; lovemaking with Roy was all but nonexistent because Roy claimed that he was afraid to touch Angie, afraid he would hurt her, she'd become so fragile. When Nancy told Roy about Angie and Jean-Georges, Roy packed his bags.

"I'm so sorry, Roy." She sobbed, her gut wrenching.

What had she done? What had she been thinking? If only she could take it back. On her knees, she reached out to him and begged him not to go, to forgive her. He turned and took her hand.

"Please get up," he said. "You look pathetic. This is embarrassing."

He pulled; her brittle twig of a wrist snapped.

"Pretty face," the doctors and nurses murmured above her as she lay on the cold slab of an ER table that night, the moon full again, beaming through the glass ceiling of the room, instruments clinging and clanging, dropping onto metal trays while the doctors put Angie back together again.

Although Angie tried to eat more, her stomach had become the size of a pea, and a pea was about all she could digest at a time. Her stomach continued to diminish, until the morning she woke up and couldn't find herself. She cried out for Roy to help look for her, but he was nowhere.

"Don't hate me!" she cried out louder. "I can't bear it." She jumped up and down on the mattress. She sobbed. She wailed. His face appeared over her; his blond beard nearly suffocated her, he was so close. Thank God he was still there. But his brown eyes were slits because he was squinting in an effort to see her, she was so tiny. She was nearly invisible.

"Can you see me, Roy?"

"Yes."

"Can you hear me?"

"Not too well. You're a little hoarse."

Of course she was hoarse. She'd been screaming so much her throat was dry and scratchy.

"What is it, Ange?"

"Cold." She was whispering now, relieved to have garnered his attention. "So cold."

"Big day today, Ange. Big day."

Happy. He was happy again. He'd forgiven her. Relieved, she waited for him to kiss her, but he scooped her up as he would some loose change and dropped her into his crisply pressed shirt pocket with the company logo. He stepped into his pants.

"Roy!" She let out a muffled cry. She had fallen into a corner of the pocket and was struggling to get on her feet.

"Are you in pain?"

She was, and it must have been because she was growing now—she was getting larger, in what was not his pocket after all but between the stiff sheets. She could see her hand on top of the blanket, inside Roy's; they were almost the same size.

"Roy—" Her jaws moved slowly in their paralytic waking stage. "I don't want to have the surgery."

His look was somewhat bewildered, but she was the one who was perplexed. He had said she could change her mind. Now maybe he had changed his.

"What are you talking about, Ange?" His words were clearer now, louder.

"Will you call Dr. Barter for me, Roy? I didn't sleep well; bad dreams—terrible dreams. I'm so tired, and my voice. Call him and tell him I changed my mind."

"Honey." His voice rose to that insistent, high pitch. He patted her forehead. He held out a plastic cup of water; the bent straw met her lips. "It was a really long surgery. There were complications. But the worst is over."

She tried hard to focus on him. He was smiling, standing tall. So tall and unsuspecting. So far away.

Comfort Me, Stranger

When Rosemary's marriage collapsed after 26 years, so did Rosemary. Where was the gutsy woman who doled out advice like antacids to the lovelorn and the confused? She had become one of her most pathetic readers: puffy eyed, long wavy hair flowing, she roamed her condo in the newly renovated jailhouse, wearing a nightgown like some unkempt mad figure in a gothic novel or a nomad who couldn't decide which room provided the best feng shui. When she did manage to sleep, she dreamt bad dreams about the beautiful home in which she'd raised her babies and had been forced to give up; about Nate moving in with his paramour and the new babies he would have with her.

Her mother blamed Rosemary for having worked too much and not having paid enough attention to Nate; Nate's mother blamed the other woman; nobody blamed Nate. Still, Rosemary had held it together long enough to move out of her home and into the former jail with the 15-inch-thick concrete walls that she seemed to have run up against. Since she seemed incapable of asking for a leave of absence from the Dear Lydia column she wrote, Rosemary's cousins banded together to take control of her life before life itself overcame their dear older cousin.

The e-mails flew out first thing every morning—cyber-space ablaze with emotion. Who had spoken with Rosemary last? Who was privy to her latest thoughts of suicide—or murder? Who had brought her food, sent her music to listen to, tranquilizers to down? What was her emotional temper-ature, which would set the tone for intervention over the next 24 hours? For six months Rosemary had monopolized their thoughts and conversations to the point of threaten-ing their relationships with their husbands, who com-plained about having to play second fiddle or who feared for the mental health of their wives who had taken on Rose-mary's suffering. (In the end this was really still their com-plaining about having to play second fiddle.)

Nancy usually started the morning e-mail chain:

> *I told her she's been an abused woman. After all,*
> > *Nate was a bully from day one. Love, Nancy*
> *Okay, I'll tell her that too when I call. We need to*
> > *be on the same page. Love, Joanna*
> *I think I've had it. Love, Barbara*
> *We need to be patient with her. Love, Angie*

They soon closed with initials only:

> *She's hapless. N (They all knew Nancy meant*
> > *hopeless.)*
> *How long can we go on pretending we're Lydia? I*
> > *was up until two am answering letters. B*
> *I was up until three. A*
> *This is crazy. N*
> *This is necessary. If she loses her job, what'll become*
> > *of her when she turns the corner? We can do it. J*

E-mailing gave way to live conversations, as they switched to Skype conference calls:

Joanna: Forget most of the letters. It's the ones that get printed in the paper that are important, the letters that have to include a recipe. That's Rosemary's, or should I say Lydia's, trademark.

Barbara: Joanna's right. What should I suggest for the man who slept with his mother-in-law?

Nancy: Arsenic.

Barbara: Seriously.

Nancy: I'm serious.

Angie: Something to cleanse his system of the toxins propelling him.

Nancy: How about a steady diet of lye?

Angie: I know. Hot lemonade. That's what my doctor used to give me for acne.

Barbara: I opt for the Drano. And tell him to soak his dick in it while he's at it.

Joanna: We're trying to save Rosemary's job, remember?

Angie: Joanna's right. Rosemary would never treat a reader like that.

Nancy: That was Rosemary's problem. She never treated Nate like that either.

Barbara: Amen.

Joanna: Nate called Elliott. He wants to play tennis. They're doubles partners, you know.

Barbara: Tell him to forget it! I told Lenny that under no uncertain circumstances is he to associate with him.

Angie: Don't you think that's a bit unrealistic?

*Nate's been in our family for a quarter century.
These things happen.
Barbara: I don't give a shit. There are ways to do
these "things" and Nate did it wrong.
To which they all agreed.
Joanna: Do you think the newspaper is onto us?
A resounding no was typed by each one.
Angie: One woman did complain about the recipe
I sent her. I thought Aunt Katie's polenta and
sausage was a perfect dish for a young bride to
serve her mother-in-law when the girl asked her
mother-in-law to move out of the couple's new
home. Only it backfired. Now the mother-in-law
thinks the daughter-in-law is too good a cook
and she doesn't want to ever leave.
Barbara: I told a man whose wife wants to divorce
him because he doesn't do his share around the
house to impress his wife with ropa vieja, and he
got pissed and wrote back saying he wasn't going
to cook anything he couldn't pronounce.
Nancy: Maybe Rosemary's really known what
she's been talking about all these years.
Joanna: I told a young man to offer his girlfriend
a trip to Italy and propose to her there, and she
would surely say yes.
Barbara: Italy. Italy. Always Italy with you.
Nancy: Did he?
Joanna: He did. How was I supposed to know he
was knee-deep in debt and his financial situation
was the reason the girl wouldn't marry him?
Nancy: How does Rosemary know when people
are hiding the truth?*

Joanna: She just has a feel for these things. Besides, she's been doing this for years. We'll get better at it.
Angie: If we don't go crazy first.
Barbara: What do I tell the kid whose father has cancer and refuses to stop smoking?
Nancy: Your father's an asshole.

***

The brunt of the burden lay on Angie, who lived closest to Rosemary. Newly married, pregnant with her first child and still holding down a full-time job, she bore witness to Rosemary's condition.

"At least get dressed, Ro," she begged her cousin. "It's nearly five."

"Why bother? Only six more hours until I go to bed again. Besides, it makes for fewer laundry days." Her voice was flat and thick and dark.

"Have you tried melatonin?"

"I've tried every sleeping pill under the sun. Forget the crunchy granola stuff."

"How about meditation? I could walk you through it."

"Shouldn't you be home making dinner?"

"Roy's cooking tonight."

"Lovely."

"You just sounded like Lauren Bacall."

"Did Lauren Bacall sound like shit? Because I feel like shit."

"I brought you some macaroni and cheese."

"Put it in the fridge, next to the chicken cacciatore."

"You still have some of that?"

"I have all of that."

"Well, I'm sorry if you didn't like it. I'm not as good a cook as you are."

"I wouldn't know."

"Rosemary, what are you surviving on?"

"Pop Tarts."

"You aren't serious?"

"The kid next door brings them to me. He sneaks them from his mother's pantry. I've been cooking for over 25 years. I'm done."

"Are you done eating too?"

Rosemary gestured to the refrigerator. The untouched meals spoke for themselves.

***

Angie was long gone when the doorbell rang. Rosemary ignored it, but whoever was in the long narrow hallway wasn't giving up. She put her pillow over her disheveled gray hair (she hadn't colored it since Nate's departure) and started repeating the Lord's Prayer. She wasn't begging for a miracle; it was just something she was in the habit of doing when she wanted to blot out anything disturbing. Still the doorbell rang. "Go away!" she cried. The caller persisted. She longed for a forklift to trundle her dead weight to the door so she could give the obsessed bell ringer hell. She rose with an effort worthy of a three-hundred-pound Lazarus. Through the peephole she saw a young man holding a chocolate cake on a platter. She was taken with the attractiveness of the cake; Angie had never brought anything so rich looking, delicately topped as it was with shavings and chopped walnuts—just like one of her own recipes. Such pains someone had taken for a fundraiser.

"I'm not buying it," she said. "I don't care what the cause."

The man rang the bell again.

Rosemary raised her volume. "I'm on a diet. I'm indigent. I'm sick. Go away."

"Please open the door, Lydia."

"Lydia?" She was taken aback. "Lydia croaked 16 years ago."

"But you are the woman who writes the column now, aren't you?"

"Not anymore."

"Then who's writing the column?"

"Who are you?"

"Avery Sloan. I live on the third floor. I'm the building engineer—you know, the super. "

"Didn't know we had one, and why are you standing at my door with a chocolate cake?"

"It's kind of a thank-you gift. It's your recipe. You gave it to me—told me to make it for my parents the night I came out to them."

"And it helped?"

"No. They haven't spoken to me since."

"Sorry." One more life ruined, along with her own, by her unprofessional counseling.

She returned to the couch. The doorbell rang again. Determined to silence this pest, Rosemary got up and opened the door this time, but before she could speak, the young man in paint-splattered jeans and a Boston Red Sox T-shirt practically shoved the cake in her face, making it impossible to close the door.

"You didn't use bittersweet chocolate," Rosemary said. "I can smell it. Maybe that's where you went wrong."

"I only had semisweet. Does it really matter?"

"Are you gay or bisexual?"

"I get the point," he said.

"Good. Now go home."

Rosemary felt something like regret about what she had just said. It was the first time since her separation she had actually felt anything at all about someone other than herself. Besides, she was intrigued by his ethereal nature. He was like a figure in a life-size El Greco painting she remembered from a visit to the Prado in Madrid. The dead man's eyes were cast downward while his elongated, dark-haired body floated on a cloud toward heaven. The eeriness of the deep eye sockets had struck Rosemary as strongly as the artist's depiction of humility, guilt, and shame in his expression.

"Well, if it's really good chocolate, semisweet could work," she said, lying. And then surprised herself and invited the slim young man with the curly black hair and beard and deep-set black eyes to come in.

"Actually," he said, "it was really the prison term that severed our relationship."

"You're an ex-con?"

"It was a short sentence."

"How short?"

"Seven years."

"My God!"

"I'm not a serial rapist or a bank robber. And I didn't serve my term in the state pen. I was right here, when the building was a correctional facility."

The choice of correctional facility did little to ease Rosemary's angst about the formerly gruesome quarters for which she owned a hefty mortgage. She should have been frightened, but other people's troubles intrigued Rosemary; it was her business.

"I want you to know that I was gay before I went in."

"That's a consolation. You wouldn't happen to be a priest, would you?"

"You must be confusing me with another reader."

Rosemary nodded. The young man took this as an invitation to sit on her couch; she did not protest. He'd suddenly risen in her estimation, since she had a soft spot for gay men. She considered them a notch above everyone else because she'd never met one she didn't like immensely.

"By the way, what's your real name? Rita? Rene? Roxanne? There's only an initial on the mailbox."

"It's Rosemary. But how did you know I was Lydia? Hardly anyone knows that. They still insist on using good ole' Lydia's 1950 photo next to the byline."

"I confess I overheard you and the blond woman talking."

"She does have a loud voice."

"You both do."

Despite his bravado, he nervously tugged on his beard the way a chess master might caress his chin while pondering the consequences of his next move.

"Have you tried tweezers? Better yet, a razor?" Rosemary said.

"Excuse me?"

"You're pulling on your beard. Don't do that. You've obviously made a habit of it."

"I wasn't aware."

"That's the thing about habits. My husband was a bad habit."

And for the first time in ages, Rosemary felt the vibrating vocal cords and rumbling in the larynx that signaled a genuine belly laugh at what she thought was a grand joke.

"Shall I cut the cake?" he asked.

*** *

Angie: He brings her chocolate ice cream nearly every day.

Nancy: He's stalking her.

Joanna: They're friends.

Barbara: He's stalking her.

Joanna: Whatever for?

Nancy: Get real. He's an ex-con—a young ex-con: money for drugs, sex.

Angie: He sounds sweet.

Nancy: Angie, sometimes you're so clueless.

Joanna: But he's gay.

Angie: He could be bi.

Nancy: Gay people don't murder? Bi people don't steal?

Barbara: She's always had a thing for gays. She's wanted one of the boys in our family to be one.

Nancy: Gays are not something that's chic to have around, like a Persian cat. They're people too, you know.

Barbara: Forget the gay thing. He's an ex-con!

Angie: What do you think he was in for?

Joanna: Seven years is a long time. Maybe embezzlement or tax evasion."

Barbara: Assault with a deadly weapon?

Angie: Maybe he's a terrorist.

Joanna: She's talking about working again.

Nancy: She's not ready.

Barbara: Well, I am. I'm sick of these people's problems and I can't think of any more recipes that are simple enough for them to handle, or not

*insulting to their ethnicity, or threatening to their
dietary restrictions. My house burned down and I'm
living in a five-room town house with Lenny and
the twins peering over my shoulder, telling me what
to write to these whiners. I have my own problems.
Nancy: Yours are temporary. And so is taking on
the column.
Joanna: Do you think we might be jealous?
Nancy: Of Rosemary having a gay friend?
Joanna: Of her having a friend who can help her
more than we can.*

***

Avery Sloan visited Rosemary several times a week: he
helped her set up her computer on the dining room table;
he hooked up her new DVD player; he painted her bedroom
lime green. He was good at high tech and low tech. He was
good at delivering the letters she'd written that had to be
mailed from the newspaper to the main office—the thought
of encountering her former colleagues was overwhelming
for Rosemary. And he did it all with an unassuming ease
that she appreciated. Her self-absorbed husband had taken
up so much space. She had learned to deal with him the
way New England towns deal with enormous amounts of
snow: she had carefully maneuvered around him, found
ways to accommodate him, and then, just like snow in
spring, she had woken up one day and he was gone.

And talking to Avery was such a pleasure. It wasn't only
that they'd read the same books and liked the same movies
and art exhibits. Their brains absorbed information the
same way: quickly, concisely, and cynically.

She walked with him in the nearby park. Round and round they went on their daily constitutional, alerting each other to stray dogs or rocks on the path or wire barriers almost invisible at night that blocked off certain areas. She began to cook again, preparing elegant dinners for him; he brought her takeout. She gave him haircuts and trimmed his beard; she didn't resume coloring her hair. (He liked it long and gray.)

He was older than her son yet substantially younger than she—somewhere in between. And that was how they saw themselves: somewhere in between wise mother and innocent son, supportive friend and charming lover. There were no sexual advances, just playful innuendo that neither of them had any intention of pursuing but, while Avery confessed when he found men attractive, Rosemary swore she'd rather have a monkey than ever live with another man. And for all he did for her, Rosemary assumed that she was filling some greater need of his, although she hadn't quite put her finger on what it was.

From time to time she brought up the prison term, but even when she asked him straight-out about his crime, he skirted the topic with a childlike giggle she found appealing. She displayed no curiosity about seeing his third-floor apartment, something she withheld from her cousins for the simple reason that there was no third floor. Barbara suggested he might be a thief, but Rosemary said she had brought nothing but the bare essentials to the condo and he was welcome to them. Joanna said he could be a gigolo looking to marry and then kill her for her estate, but Rosemary knew that, if that had been the case, he would have been too eager to invade her space, and intolerant of the considerable privacy they allowed between them.

One day he appeared at her door with an amber amulet he'd bought on the streets of New York from a Haitian voodoo priest who swore it would improve circulation and therefore bring blood to the crown and lift the spirit. Another time he brought her a canister of health powder that, when mixed with juice, produced an emerald green drink with deeper green strands floating in it.

"I'm not going to be craving raw liver next, am I?" she asked. "I'm warning you, I'm beyond childbearing. The movie title is where the similarity ends."

"It's proven to increase stamina 45 percent. And there were no gargoyles on this building last time I looked. It was a great read though, wasn't it? I finished *Rosemary's Baby* in one night when I was in fifth grade."

"You shouldn't have. It's inappropriate reading for a ten-year-old."

She drank the drink every day, nearly gagging on its vilely bitter taste. She chased it with crackers or fruit, and sometimes had to brush her teeth to get rid of the taste. Within several weeks, however, she had no more desire to sleep most of the day. In fact, she had more energy than she remembered ever having. She returned to the health club. She took up flamenco dancing.

None of the other condo tenants seemed to notice Avery. It was as though, when Rosemary walked with him, he was invisible. She even started to doubt his existence.

"You aren't the soul of some poor tortured prisoner who was beaten to death or found hanging from a light fixture with a piece of cord he'd made from bits of gristle he saved over 30 years and tied together, are you?"

Avery just laughed.

She resisted the temptation to Google him. It would have been such an easy thing to do. After all, he had eavesdropped on her conversations. She'd spent a third of her life urging others to open their eyes and see beyond their own assumptions, because assumptions were often just that, born from needs, oblivious to mine fields or "red flags," to quote a phrase she liked to use. Unfortunately, people made life-determining decisions based on those narrowly focused, self-centered assumptions. Unlike Barbara and Joanna, she didn't believe in ghosts or reincarnation; one lifetime was time enough to pay back bad deeds. She did believe in karma, though—that what you sowed was what you reaped, what went around came around. As for Avery's uncanny resemblance to the 400-year-old El Greco spirit she'd seen, everyone knew the painter's work was a product of his astigmatism.

***

As Rosemary grew stronger and cognizant of things beyond herself (her cousins said she "returned to this earth"), she realized that, when her cousins decided to visit, they would not only want to meet Avery but would try to see his apartment. Nancy felt that the way a person kept their home told all about them; Barbara was passionate about decorating and believed that gays had a knack for interior design. They would grill him on every detail of his existence. Rosemary had suggested they go out to lunch, but Barbara insisted on eating in, no doubt hoping to run into Avery. Rosemary, however, would not subject Avery to their scrutiny. Nor would she subject her own happiness to the possibility of it being deemed a figment of her imagination, something she had created in her subconscious to help her go on, because she was, and must continue to be, the reliable, the wise, the immortal Dear Lydia. But there was no dissuading the determined women who traveled from their various locales and showed up at her door in a snowstorm, bearing homemade chicken tetrazzini, fennel salad, and blueberry-topped cheesecake, and demanding to meet Avery Sloan.

"I've invited him for dessert," Rosemary said. "And I don't know why you insisted on bringing food. God knows you've done enough for me. I wanted to cook for you."

"He's coming for dessert. Perfect," Joanna said. "That will give us time alone first."

"You look great, Rose. So much better than the last time we saw you," Nancy said.

"You're back in the saddle," Barbara said.

"I hate that expression," Angie said.

"Why?" Joanna asked.

"I just do. It's crude."

"Sexual repression," Nancy told Angie, whose hands cradled a belly now in its seventh month. "Wouldn't you say, Lydia?" Nancy turned to Rosemary.

"I have to admit the thought of us sitting in someone's prison cell kind of gives me the creeps," Joanna said, looking around.

"Here's something to give you the creeps; Lenny told me that Nate and his girlfriend are getting married," Barbara said. "She's pregnant."

Avery showed up not a minute too early, or late, in a pair of khakis and a light blue shirt opened at the neck to let a clump of black chest hair peek through—a departure from his usual attire. In contrast, his hair was a bit wiry and out of control, and so he seemed like a schoolboy who had stood impatiently while his mother had groomed him and then run before she was quite finished. The creases in the corners of the eyes that matched the color of his shirt added maturity to his demeanor. He carried a bottle of Prosecco, which, after the introductions were made, he took to the kitchen and returned with it on a tray along with six champagne glasses. That he knew his way around Rosemary's condo was an understatement; he was downright comfortable, the women's glances said.

They all, with the exception of pregnant Angie, drank to Rosemary, to cousins—and to friends. Nancy wasted no time in asking where his apartment was, and Rosemary braced herself. She hoped he would at least have the wit to lower the floor number, but she was unprepared for his announcement that he lived secretly in the basement, attempting to conserve what was left of a paltry inheritance from his grandmother.

"How do you get in?" Nancy asked, knowing the doors were always locked.

"You'd be surprised how many people have no idea who their neighbors are. Show your face enough and they hold the door for you."

"So you're not an ex-con?" Joanna asked.

"I bet you're not even gay," Angie added, a little disappointed.

"I'm all those things," Avery insisted. "I'm just not the super, and I don't have a proper place to live. And if you ladies wish to roll me up in this Oriental carpet and drop me out the window and into the dumpster, I'll understand."

"In other words, you're homeless," Joanna said sympathetically.

"Where do you shower?" Angie asked.

"Who the fuck are you?" Rosemary stared at him long and hard.

He cleared his throat. "My grandmother was born Eugenia Sirkowsky."

Rosemary gasped.

"And ours was Concetta Capolavoro," Nancy said. "So what?"

"His grandmother was Lydia," Rosemary explained.

"You can see why they changed her name for the column," Avery said. "And I sneak into the fitness room downstairs to shower."

They were not amused.

"But everything else is true. I did serve seven years in this jail," he offered proudly.

They all, speaking at the same time, asked questions ranging from what had he been in for and how much his inheritance was to why he was hanging around Rosemary.

"I still don't understand what you want with Rosemary." Angie repeated her question clearly and loudly.

And while the others pursed their lips at her naiveté, they too had no idea what he wanted with Rosemary.

"You never overheard any of my conversations with Angie, did you?" Rosemary asked.

"I wrote to you right after you took over the column after my grandmother died. I was 25 and still hadn't come out to my parents. I should have told my grandmother, but —well—she was my grandmother and, by the time I was ready, she was gone. Sometimes it's easier to talk to a stranger. Sometimes a stranger is all you have. And your letter was so kind and encouraging, and you did send me the chocolate cake recipe and I tried it, and it failed. When I went to jail, my parents really shut the door on me. But I've always been grateful to you for being there for me, and when I read your divorce decree in the paper—"

"You read about my divorce?" Rosemary asked warily.

"Yes." He lowered his head as though he could not admit this to her face.

"So you have been stalking her!" Nancy leaned in toward him.

"I've kept track of her. That's all."

"He hasn't stalked me," Rosemary said. "He's never stalked me."

"I think it might be time for us to leave," Joanna said.

"We're going to leave her here with him?" Nancy said.

"We're going to leave." Barbara took her hand.

"I'll call you tonight," Angie said.

"We'll all call," Joanna said.

***

"I have one question for you, Avery. If that is your name," Rosemary said when they were alone.

"It is ..."

"Why did you lie?"

"You needed me to."

"I beg your pardon?"

"You knew I didn't live here, Rosemary. When I made that slip about the third floor, you never questioned me. You've never asked to see my place. You're the most intuitive person I've ever known, except maybe for my grandmother. Sometimes fantasy helps us maneuver through reality—ask any ex-con."

"And you think I wouldn't have befriended you if you had told me your real circumstances?"

"Honestly?"

"We need to start somewhere."

"No, I don't think you would have. When I read your column, I could tell that something was very wrong, that you weren't writing those letters. And if you were hurting, you must be hiding from people you knew—and anyone related to them. I know what it's like to lose someone's trust. You needed a stranger."

"But why, Avery?"

"I just told you."

"Not the lies. Why were you so interested in me in the first place?"

"You were there for me when no one else was. I was grateful, and I wanted to reciprocate. All right, I needed to. I suppose there was a selfish part in it—helping you helped me too. I needed a purpose."

She understood this: having been asked to take over Lydia's column had salvaged years of her inability to carve out a satisfying career for herself. (She had worked as a realtor, a bank teller, a reporter on police logs, and hated each job.) It had finally given her a suitable identity—albeit someone else's. Helping troubled others had been Rosemary's claim to fame, her salvation. The evening Nate had announced he was leaving, at the King of Siam restaurant, she believed that her amateurish advice over the past ten years had been as great a sham as her marriage. Who else's life, besides her own, had she so badly misdiagnosed? How many other desperate souls' messages had flown below her radar while she played psychologist?

"Nothing's really different," Avery insisted. "I just don't really live here. What's the big deal?"

At one time in her self-righteous life it would have been a very big deal. But a man's deceit had plunged her into the pit of misery, and now a man's deceit had pulled her out.

"I should have told my grandmother I was gay before she died. Then again, she was sharp like you, Rosemary. She probably always knew."

But then Lydia would have said something, Rosemary thought. She would have eased her grandson's pain if Avery had really been her grandson. She knew that there had never been a divorce decree listed in any newspaper. What surprised her was that she didn't care. What was true was that he had helped her. Perhaps sometimes—just some-times—people might need to fortify themselves by averting their eyes to what they see most clearly and feel most strongly.

"They're looking for a receptionist at the newspaper. I'm pretty sure I can persuade them to overlook your 'crim-inal' background; it's not exactly CIA work. Besides, we have a liberal slant. This is a two-bedroom. I wouldn't mind your staying for a while, until you get your feet on the ground. Actually, I think I'd enjoy the company. But you'd have to sleep on the floor when my children visit, and I in-sist you share all the chores."

"I look forward to it." He relaxed his shoulders and settled back into the easy chair like a man of his grand-mother's era, who had just returned from a hard day at the office and was about to light a pipe. "I'd like to tell you what I did—what they convicted me of."

Rosemary held up her hand to silence him. "Not right now. Not just yet."

His eyes widened with surprise.

"Let me bask a bit in relief, Avery. I must say, for a while I thought you might be a figment of my imagination or not of this world. You are something of an angel to me."

He laughed, that childlike giggle of his she so enjoyed.

"Don't laugh. These things happen. Take my ex-husband's girlfriend. She's pregnant, you know—by the devil himself."

Forecast for a Sunny Day

"**D**id you see him?" Marco Ficola asked his daughter. They sat side by side, separated by the contraptions engineers design to shift gears and hold coffee cups and cigarette butts.

"Who?" Joanna fastened her seat belt and placed the key in the ignition.

"The owner of the villa in Gronda. Did you see him when you were there last year?"

Joanna began to maneuver out of her parking place; her mother's face, chalky and seemingly more wrinkled than the day before, filled the rearview mirror.

"Ma, can you move your head, please?"

"What?"

"Your head. Can you move it to one side? I can't see the car behind me."

"What is she saying?" Myra Ficola asked her husband, as though Joanna was speaking a foreign language.

"Take your hat off!" Marco Ficola bellowed. "She lost her hearing aid again. Can't remember where she put a two-thousand-dollar hearing aid. Can you imagine?"

"What are you telling her?" Myra Ficola said in an equally loud voice. Joanna longed for a volume control button.

"I don't know why you have to wear that damned huge hat all the time." Marco's shouting had brought on a coughing fit.

"I don't want to catch a chill. I read that you should always wear something on your head. That's where you lose most of your body heat. That's probably why you can't get rid of this thing you have. You never wear a hat."

"For cryin' out loud, Piovoso said it's going to be sunny, sixty degrees today."

"Piovoso said. What does he know?"

"He's a meteorologist. He knows."

"What does he know," Marco said mimicking his wife. Then, waiting to be sure his cough was in check, he let out a sign of exasperation. "She believes everything she reads. She reads too damn much."

"At least she still reads." This was a jab at her father, who had given up his beloved newspapers and novels, claiming he could no longer focus.

There was a time when Joanna's mother would have told him to shut up and stop making fun of her; there was a time when he wouldn't have ridiculed her so much, when they operated on a more even playing field. But she could hardly hear now, and so he was free to vent all he liked, particularly when he had his back to her. She was shrinking a bit more each day and her voice becoming frailer. Joanna didn't know for whom to feel sorrier: her mother, who couldn't hear or remember what she had eaten for lunch five minutes after she'd consumed it, or an anxiety-ridden father whose patience had become tissue-paper thin.

"Joanna, I asked you if you saw him," her father said. "You didn't answer me."

"Dad, I don't know who you're talking about."

"Oh, come on, Joanna. Don't play dumb. I told you about him."

"You did?"

"Of course. He was the owner of Villa Foresta." He tilted his head and shouted into the backseat. "Myra, remember Harlan Bigwood?"

"Didn't he play for the Patriots?"

"Myra, he was the owner of the villa we found the last time we were in Italy."

"Oh yes. The New Zealand man with the large wife."

"That's it!" He was thrilled that she remembered. He would have kissed her had she not been sitting behind him.

This was how they spent their time, Joanna thought. No wonder they weren't bored—it took so long for their decaying minds to unravel everything. He wasn't always this cantankerous or she this zany; they had their good days, when they discussed the upcoming presidential election, the Hallmark movie they had just seen on TV, the sermon Father Ryan had given on Sunday.

"Maybe you told Elliott about it," Joanna said, referring to her husband.

"I told *you*."

Maybe her father had. Maybe she was becoming like her mother, her life slowly getting caught between the slippery folds of her brain. She suddenly felt remorse for her own lack of tolerance. She'd quit talking to her parents—really talking; it just took too much effort. It was easier to phone the doctor herself or to send the thank-you notes, rather than explain to them what had to be done. She had been that way with her daughter, but Myra had told Joanna that if she didn't let Jill do things on her own, how was she to learn? Well, Joanna's parents didn't need to learn anymore, so why did she have to humor them? Time was running out for her too.

"I don't know why you always have to come with us to the doctor, Joanna," her mother said. "Your father is perfectly capable of driving."

"Please stop interrupting, Myra. I'm trying to ask our daughter a question, but she keeps avoiding me."

"I'm not avoiding you." Joanna was laughing now. "How could anyone avoid you, Dad?"

This statement offended him; he knew it was not meant as a compliment, so he turned sullen, his body sinking into his car seat.

"It was a joke, Dad."

"Yeah."

***

"How are you feeling, Mr. Ficola?" Dr. Adler asked, looking not at Marco but at his chart.

"I'm fine. I don't even know why I'm here. At my age, if you look for something, you're going to find it. I have a lot of symptoms—comes with the territory. I told you, I'm good —good to go."

"Dad, tell him about your cough and—"

"I brought my mother," Marco said sarcastically, interrupting Joanna, who sat with a notebook on her lap.

"The cough still keeping you up at night?" Dr. Adler asked the chart.

"I get up so many times to go to the bathroom, I don't know which keeps me up. How about you give me another antibiotic? I can shake this thing. I licked typhoid fever during the war, I licked pneumonia last year, and I can lick this."

"You've already been on two antibiotics. That's why Dr. Mathas sent you to me."

"Enough of the chitchat. What did my test show, doctor?"

"Your CAT scan confirmed my suspicions. You have adenocarcinoma."

"And that's—?"

"Lung cancer," Dr. Adler said without changing his expression or intonation. He said everything matter-of-factly, as though he were hooked up to an IV of ice water. "Most likely from the smoking."

"I quit 15 years ago."

"You smoked for 45."

That last remark silenced the mighty Marco Ficola. Joanna had never seen her father at a loss for words. His eyes filled with disbelief. When they told him Joanna's daughter Jill had died, he had broken down and wept and cursed God. But now, confronting his own mortality, he sat in shock. Joanna decided they'd get a second opinion. She didn't like Dr. Adler.

"I'm sorry about the diagnosis, but this is what you have to do now." This was routine for Dr. Adler, who was running a tape he'd run many times before. Joanna put down her pen, and wondered how this man could get up in the morning, have his coffee, and set out to play the Grim Reaper every day.

"We'll need a biopsy to confirm the cell type and the staging, to see how far it's spread."

"What about surgery?" Joanna managed to say.

"Depends on how advanced the cancer is. I doubt it will be an option. I'll recommend an oncologist, and she'll prescribe medical treatment. My guess is that it's at the point where there can be no remission. It's all about stabilizing it at the original site. There are certain protocols; it's a matter of your oncologist opting for a better outcome or quality of life. But I'll leave that for her."

You're damned right you will, Joanna wanted to say. We don't like your conjectures.

As though someone had snapped fingers, Marco emerged from his trance.

"So what now?" Dr. Adler's last statement had escaped him.

"There'll be more scans of your body to see how far it's spread."

Marco's last defenses crumbled. He had no more bravado. "Well. I see."

"He's okay? The chest was clear?" Myra asked Joanna.

"No, Ma."

"Oh." Her voice trailed off, her eyes welled up.

The couple left the office arm in arm, their gait slowed by a decade. Dr. Adler held Joanna back.

"The age of course is a double-edged sword. The cancer grows more slowly, but the organs are weaker, function less efficiently. They can put up with only so much treatment."

She nodded.

"You'll need to make plans. It's clear that your mother isn't capable."

"Of course." Her father was the caretaker—the keeper of pills and appointments, he was his wife's chauffeur, delivery boy, and personal shopper.

From a plastic rack on the wall, Dr. Adler removed a pamphlet with a list of names and numbers and chanted another litany: "Visiting nurses, in-home care, Catholic Charities, hospice."

"Hospice?"

"Not yet, but you need to be thinking about it. Does he have a living will?"

"Yes."

"Get it to me."

Joanna carried her resentment for this little man in the long white coat with the big name tag out to the enormous parking lot. There she stood without the faintest notion of where she had parked.

"It's way down that third row over there." Marco pointed to his left.

"I don't think so."

"Joanna, I'm telling you, it's down there."

He was right, of course. And the fact that his memory surpassed hers terrified her. Or was it that she couldn't go through it all again—a funeral, an adjustment, the emptiness only four years after having lost Jill? Twenty years from now would still be too soon. And then there was her mother to worry about. Joanna's father might have just been handed a death sentence, yet the person she felt sorriest for was herself.

***

"Well, it's been a good run," Marco said, breaking the silence on the ride home. He stared out the windshield; he saw nothing.

"It's not over, Dad. We'll get a second opinion." The flatness of their voices bounced words between them like a ping-pong ball hit in slow motion.

"My father used to say that if you're afraid to die, you don't deserve to live. I've lived my life, Joanna. I would have given it four years ago, if I could have to save Jill's."

"Don't, Dad." It wasn't the first time he'd made this impossible offer.

"Listen, Joanna." He whispered now, to make absolutely sure his wife couldn't hear. "What's she gonna do? She can't manage alone. You don't know the extent of it—how I cover for her, what I hide from everyone. Gets worse and worse every day. I don't care for myself. But what's she gonna do?"

"You know I'll take care of her. But Dad, it's not the end; there are other specialists and treatments. Besides—it's never really over."

"No, no." He shook his head. "Don't start that. I don't believe in any hereafter, if that's what you're getting at. What happens to us when we die? We go into the ground, period. That's it. That's it for all of us."

"Yet you go to church."

"For your mother. That's all. For her."

"I don't believe in that kind of hereafter either, Dad. You know I stopped believing a long time ago. But I do believe—I know—the spirit lives on in another form, another body."

"And what if it does? Is that spirit gonna cook for your mother? Is he gonna put the toothpaste on her brush in the morning? Is he gonna kiss her good night?" He was getting worked up now, his voice growing louder, and Joanna feared that soon her mother would demand to have their conversation explained to her. And Joanna would lose it then—she'd have to pull over to the side of the road and break down at the sadness of it all, because she could feel the weight of emotion in her throat.

Though he disregarded his feelings at times, Marco was not an ignorant or an insensitive man. The color had drained from Joanna's face, and she blinked rapidly to see through tearing eyes. Her anguish touched him; he lowered his voice.

"You really think that about the spirit?" His tone was considerate, respectful.

"I know so," she said, grateful for the opportunity to salvage her composure and eager to tell him about the little girl she had met at Villa Foresta the year before, but she held back. There had been far too much shocking news revealed on this sunny day.

"You never told me whether you saw the owner of the villa." Her father returned the conversation to her last trip to Italy, as though he had read her mind. He was looking at her now, searching for an answer.

"The owners weren't there, but I know that they're from Naples and that they recently bought the villa from a New Zealand couple."

"He's dead. I knew it." Marco turned melancholy.

"Oh, I don't know if we're even talking about the same person. I just know that that couple doesn't own the villa any longer."

"He would never have given up the place unless he had to. He had cancer." Marco coughed, but it was a cough of discomfort, an attempt to cover up a quivering voice that could barely speak the word that had taken on a life of its own inside his body.

"How do you know?"

"He told me that day your mother and I stopped there while we were driving around the countryside. He was thrilled to have someone to talk English to yet someone who also belonged to Italy. Sometimes two people just hit it off. We sat in his restaurant and drank wine for hours."

"Restaurant? There wasn't any restaurant when we were there. No one was there except a caretaker-concierge-cook all rolled into one." Thinking about the villa, she became animated.

"And he didn't tell you about Harlan?" He cleared his throat of phlegm and turned toward the back seat. In the rearview mirror, Joanna saw what her father was looking around to confirm: Myra's eyes were closed; her head rested on one side as her lips muttered sleep garble.

"No."

"A dynamic man. Very tall, strong. Good looking. Engaging." He became more excited with each word, and Joanna could swear her father was smitten with this person. She had never heard him pay this kind of tribute to another man, let alone one outside the family.

"Worked for an international relief organization. Traveled the world. He was passionate about rebuilding that villa. Didn't know a damned thing about construction though. He was arguing with the workers while I was there about that long flight of stairs that leads to the parking lot. I knew he was all wrong about the pitch but I didn't say anything."

"The stairs are falling apart, cracked all over."

Marco let out a roar of satisfaction.

"Figures. I knew that would happen. A stubborn man. Said he would finish that villa even it killed him. Said he wanted to be buried there."

"He is—under those stairs." Joanna remembered Paolo telling her that at breakfast. She remembered the firm grip that had held her down when she had tried to run off with Elisabetta. Marco, caught up in his own reverie, ignored her last statement.

"He said he didn't want to die until he saw his son kick his drug habit, too. He was a real fighter."

"Did you see the son?" Joanna was quick to ask.

"No. He was in New Zealand at the time. He came and went. They all did."

Joanna hesitated to tell her father what she was about to reveal, but in view of the news he had received and the story he had just shared, he was more vulnerable than she had ever seen him. And she needed to tell him. She couldn't think of him leaving this world without knowing.

"I met a little girl at the villa, Dad. You're going to think this is crazy. Her mother is the cleaning woman. The caretaker said her father was a drug addict—the owner of the villa's son. Dad, I believe she's Jill."

Like a cowering puppy expecting to be reprimanded with a smack on the head, she waited for her father's reaction.

"So that's why you believe. That's what all the reincarnation talk is about?"

"Yes."

"What makes you think it was Jill?" His interest was genuine.

"She was born three days after Jill died. She was playing with a miniature wooden horse. You know how much Jill loved horses. She even looked like Jill. Dad, it's like you said about Harlan being dead: I just knew."

"And Elliott?"

"My husband is a man of science."

"You weren't kidding when you came home and said you had a good trip."

Joanna couldn't contain the smile that broke over her face.

"The day I met him," Marco said, "we sat and talked until dark. I had taken your mother back to my brother's to rest. You know how easily she gets tired. Besides, she didn't cotton to his wife—who, by the way, he later told me, hated Italy and had a boyfriend back in New Zealand. Your mother has good intuitions; she can sense these things. I went back to the villa that evening. There was something about the guy—we came from different parts of the world but we got along so well, and I had the feeling that maybe we'd met before. But of course we hadn't. I guess I saw a little of myself in him—for better or worse."

"What do you mean?"

"I know my strengths, Joanna, and my weaknesses. I know my fears have led me to walk a straight line in my life —be precise, follow through—but I'm also aware of how inflexible they've made me. I like to be right. Actually, I think I am right most of the time."

"You're right more than you're wrong, Dad. But you are wrong sometimes," she pointed out. She really wanted to know if something intimate had happened between her father and this stranger, but there was no way to ask. "So, how did you leave each other? Did you agree to keep in touch?"

"We never talked about that. It wasn't a subject. There was only that day. And if another time happened to us—if I had been lucky enough to get in another trip back to my homeland—maybe I would have tried to find him again."

"Maybe?"

"Some things are better left alone. They aren't meant to be built on. They are what they are. *Hai capito?*"

She said she understood, even though her father had just spoken of a man as he might have an exotic woman with whom he'd had a tryst, a lover who had opened up a world of mysteries so profound that their ramifications were too overwhelming to speculate about. She said she understood because that was what you said to her father when he asked that, because he wasn't really asking—he was ordering you not to rock the boat, to leave well enough alone. He was closing a door, and there was to be no more knocking on it. That was how he dealt with his fear. And that was why she now knew for certain that he had never before spoken about the owner of the villa.

Joanna glanced into the rearview mirror. Her mother was still dozing. Her father continued to process the notion that his granddaughter lived on as the granddaughter of a man with whom he seemed to have been infatuated. Had it been any other man, her father would never even have entertained the idea, but that it might be this man gave it some validity, and suddenly he did the extraordinary: he opened the door again.

"I had a dream last night," he confessed. "I never dream, you have to understand. At least I don't remember my dreams if I do. But last night I went back to Italy, back to the villa. He and I were sitting on the terrace looking out at the vast sky and those green hills, and I kept telling him I thought I had cancer too. We were speaking in Italian in my dream, although he didn't really speak Italian. He was speaking beautiful Italian. He never looked at me. It was like I wasn't there. I finally threw up my hands and cried out: 'Why me? Why me? *Ma perchè?* Answer me, goddammit!' That's when he turned and looked at me as though I was crazy and gave me my answer."

"Which was?"

"'Why not?' he said, as smooth and cold as ice. 'Why not?' But it wasn't him talking—it was me, me in his body, that I watched creep back into the villa with all the humility only a dead man is capable of possessing."

"You think he came to you, Dad?"

Her father grew somber again; death was no longer an entertaining guest among them. Staring blankly once more out the windshield, he shrugged the deflated shoulders that had once carried Joanna and that, so long ago, she thought were mighty enough to carry the world.

"I don't believe in coincidences, Dad. I believe that this man came to you to help you. Just as I believe that that little girl was his granddaughter—and yours."

That her father did not refute her statement was the best he could do, the closest he could come to acceptance. Suddenly none of it seemed of much importance to him —not Harlan and their relationship, not even the fact that Jill might have been reincarnated. He was far beyond that. His brittle morning anxiety had given way to stoic calm. The secret was out, the greatest mystery of his life solved. Marco had crossed over to join those who know what everyone longs and yet fears to discover: the end to his story.

"Myra, we're home," he tenderly called to his wife. "Wake up, dear."

"Already? That was so quick. All that talking you two were doing put me to sleep."

"We were speaking about Harlan Bigwood again," he said.

"Isn't he the weatherman on Channel four?"

Marco gave an exhausted sigh of compassion for his wife as he looked over at Joanna, and their knowing eyes locked in an embrace that erased all fears and their demands —at least for the moment.

"Why not, dear?" he told his wife, his gaze still fixed on his daughter. "Why not?"

Dressed to Die

On the morning of Marco Ficola's death, Myra goes to the hall closet where, for years before dementia set in, she kept her special outfits. She wore them to weddings and christenings, to church on Sunday; the red suit never failed to draw compliments from other parishioners. Always so well dressed, they said, in an era when the act of dressing up had not just relaxed but collapsed, with shorts and jeans now considered normal attire at Mass. When her mind began to wander in and out of the moment, Marco selected something for her.

"You might want to wear the black one," Joanna tells her mother, who removes a periwinkle A-line dress and matching jacket. A handwritten note is pinned onto the lapel: For my funeral.

"But this is the one I've been saving."

"For your own funeral, Ma. Not Dad's."

"Well, I just died," Myra says, in an instant of utter lucidity.

She had stopped attending Mass that last year, the year of Marco's downward spiral. While the sweet little black hospice girl, as Marco liked to call her, cared for him, Myra busied herself around the house, making coffee for nonexistent guests or finding herself lost in the kitchen when visitors actually arrived. Occasionally she demanded to be taken to the North End in Boston, where her little girl, Joanna, was waiting for her, when in fact, Joanna had moved with them from the North End to outlying Medford 35 years before. However, there were times, like now, when Myra's comprehension was undeniable, when she looked at her weakened husband and Joanna could see their years together unscrolling before her mother's eyes. These were times when love worked its magic and her mental decline did an about-face, as on the day Marco had climbed the stairs alone, at his insistence, with every effort his cancer-ridden body could put forth, and took to his bed, where he remained until his death.

"I think it's time you started looking around," Marco told his wife.

"For what?" Myra asked.

"For someone new."

Joanna was dumbfounded by the remark. Her father was not a practical joker, and she knew there was no sarcasm in his statement. Feeling like an intruder, she left the room, but aware of her mother's limited rationality and afraid she might miss her father's last breath, she left the door open and planted herself on the other side of the jamb.

"Look for someone else?" her mother said. "At my age? Don't be an old fool."

"I'm serious, *ninfa*. I don't like to think of you without a man's love."

Ninfa? Joanna had never heard her father address her mother as a nymph. He was delirious, Joanna concluded, and perhaps referring to an old flame—or maybe one not so old. The end was imminent, and Joanna only hoped her mother hadn't understood enough to be faced with painful revelations at this late date.

"You're out of your mind, Adone." Adonis!

"With love for you."

"Adone, you won't forget the promise."

"It's that time, isn't it? I won't forget, *amore. Ti prometto.*"

Now he was telling her how much he loved her and that she had always been his only love. But he was speaking in Italian, which Myra, a Polish Jew before her conversion to Catholicism, had never quite mastered. Still, she answered him in Italian, telling him that she also loved him, her Adonis, and then she bent over the bed and kissed him long on the lips, her head trembling. Joanna had never seen her parents so intimate; the Ficola men frowned on displays of affection as offensive to others and signs of weakness. Joanna's parents now presented a singular tableau, a window on over half a century of togetherness. And what was this promise they talked about? What could her father possibly promise to do for her mother, when he was a breath away from death? Joanna should have been moved to tears, but instead laughter escaped her lips like air out of a punctured balloon. It was not a laugh of derision or even of jealousy. (She and her father had always enjoyed a special bond, often at her mother's expense.) No, it was a laugh of sheer delight and gratitude for discovering that she had been wrong about her parents and their marriage all these years. There had been passion, possibly even heightened by an indiscretion. She had been so wrong, and the laughter, after all these months of tension, felt good.

"*Stai zitto!*" Be quiet! Her father chastised her for her outburst. A broad smile broke out on her mother's round face, its delicate skin seasoned with creases and two large brown spots. Her father let out what would be the last attempt at a chuckle, followed by a labored gasp for air, payment for the jocularity.

***

Joanna's husband, Elliott, takes on the task of informing relatives and friends of Marco's passing. Joanna's cousin Nancy is hanging curtains when the phone rings. She's standing on a ladder, her back to the bed, while her son Pierre uses the king-sized mattress for a trampoline. She doesn't want to wait until the curtains are up before she stops him. Besides, she has to teach him this isn't acceptable behavior.

She gathers up the yards of fabric along with the rod and descends the ladder, careful not to trip on the cloth. Draping the curtains over a chair, she positions herself in front of Pierre and tries to stop him, but the grinning boy is having so much fun she can barely slow him. She cups his fleshy face in the palms of her hands and stares directly into it. Clearly and slowly she pronounces the words: "No jumping on the bed."

"But Uncle Marco likes it!" His squirms to wriggle out of her grasp and resumes bouncing, his belly convulsing with pleasure with every giggle he lets out.

"What?" As often happens, she's misunderstood the slurred speech of a deaf boy who is being taught to communicate orally.

He turns his gaze slightly upward, appearing to be smiling at nothing. She brings the smooth cheeks opposite hers again, signaling for him to focus on her mouth. She is set on teaching Pierre to speak; each morning he attends kindergarten at a renowned school for the deaf that uses only this method. She is fearful that his inability to hear will put him at a disadvantage in life. "There are times everyone must learn what comes naturally to Pierre, and ignore what they hear—forget," her Uncle Marco once told her. "How else would family survive?"

"What did you say?" she asks Pierre again, having corralled his attention.

"Uncle Marco likes it." There is no mistaking his words this time.

"What do you mean?"

"He's here, jumping with me on the bed."

When the phone on the nightstand sounds, she sets the boy free. The call comes as no surprise.

"I have some bad news," Elliott tells her.

"I know. When?"

"Early this morning, around six."

***

After she hangs up with Elliott, Nancy calls her cousin Barbara to tell her of their Uncle Marco's death. Barbara worries that her father, Marco's older brother Joe, is too feeble to make the drive from New Jersey to Boston to bury the first of the six Ficola brothers to die.

"His legs swell, Nancy, and he has to stop so often to pee, and with all that traffic slowing us down, he's afraid there won't be a rest stop when he needs it."

"For God's sake, he's a man," Nancy says. "He can pee anywhere."

"He's a Ficola man. They only pee in a toilet—a men's toilet, or urinal, as the case may be. Once he was about to explode and still he wouldn't use the ladies' room in a pizzeria. They're proud."

"They're stubborn. Find a way. Bring an old coffee can. Do something. He has to come. He'll regret it if he doesn't."

"It'd be easier if Lenny was here. Lenny is good with him."

No, it wouldn't. It wouldn't be at all good if Lenny were there. Right now Joe Ficola can't stand the thought of his son-in-law, let alone the sight of him, but Nancy does not say this to Barbara because, in her broken heart, Barbara already knows.

Barbara's husband, Lenny, is in New Mexico, living and working for a time on his college roommate's pinto bean farm, partly to help pay his children's college tuition but mainly because he can't face the scrutiny of family and friends back east. The most successful of the cousins' husbands, Lenny had become greedy, subject to illusions of grandeur, and had assumed the lifestyle of the wealthy clients whose money he managed, sinking his family into insurmountable debt. When the economy took a nosedive, Lenny literally lost the ranch—the house he'd rebuilt on a larger lot, in a more lavish style, than the one that had burned down—and everything else they owned, along with his professional reputation. Barbara moved in with her parents, while she took steps to become recertified in the school system. In the interim, never completely down on her luck, she landed a position at the public library as a substitute for the reference librarian on maternity leave.

"I can't understand it. How could he have let this happen?" Joe repeatedly asked his brother Marco when he first found out. He spent his days conjuring up explanations, ranging from a mistress to insanity, that might have led his son-in-law to indulge in such irresponsible behavior. Over and over an embittered Joe demanded agreement on his theories from Marco, who listened but refused to speculate about Lenny's motives and who, bereft of a grandchild and battling cancer, never compared the magnitude of his grief with his brother's.

Joe has no intention of missing his baby brother's funeral. An empty Medaglia D'Oro can at his side, he and his Yankee wife get into Barbara's back seat and set out on the New Jersey Turnpike.

"It'll be good to be back in Massachusetts," observes Norma, a crusty New Englander who refuses to dye her hair like her sisters-in-law and wears little makeup. "Better off" is usually her response to the news of someone's death. It isn't so much what she says as the coldness with which she says it that has chilled her relationship with the Ficolas over the years.

"How can you say a thing like that at a time like this?" Joe asks his wife. "He was my brother. I'm in mourning, for your information."

"I didn't mean the occasion was a happy one. For heaven's sake, Joe. I only meant—."

"I know what you meant. I'm sorry."

The apologies come as a surprise to Barbara, who thinks death is a cruel teacher, a bitter dose of medicine to mellow both the frigid and the grumpy.

"I hope Rosemary doesn't bring that boyfriend of hers," Norma says.

"Avery is not her boyfriend, and why do you care?" Barbara asks.

"If he's not her boyfriend, then all the more reason for him not to be there," Norma says. "I heard her own children won't be able to make it. This is a family matter. He isn't family. Besides, he gives me the willies."

"Because he's gay?" Barbara asks, vexed.

"No, Barbara, I don't care about that. It's that other business he's hiding."

Myra is referring to Avery's lengthy prison term for a crime to which the family is still not privy nor can they research it, since Rosemary won't reveal Avery's last name.

***

They can't shut the lights off on Marco Ficola's car. One of Barbara's twins has driven it to Medford from his college in upstate New York.

His Uncle Marco had sold Matthew the car for one dollar. He had sold it rather than given it to Matthew so that, God forbid, if anything ever happened to Matthew while he was in the car, it wouldn't have anything to do with Marco having passed on bad luck. Barbara hadn't given Matthew any knives for his new apartment, either; she sold him a set for a penny. In this family superstitions have been passed down through the generations: no shoes on the table (even new ones in their boxes); no opening umbrellas inside the house; no bestowing compliments without invoking God's blessing. And while Barbara and her cousins would prefer not to observe these paganisms, they cannot ignore them—just in case there might be some truth to them.

Marco had bought the new car with a sunroof and leather seats just before he fell ill. He had never been an extravagant man; he simply wanted this car, and had finally allowed himself to indulge. Before long, however, Marco found himself being driven in it to doctors' appointments and chemotherapy and radiation treatments. And so, his only grandchild dead, he sold the car for one dollar to his brother's grandson.

Elliott spends an hour parked in front of the Ficola house, trying to turn off the lights. He wants to smash them with a tire iron, when he recalls how much his father-in-law loved the car. "Big deal. Let them burn out," he tells Matthew. "I'll buy you a new battery."

"Yes, let them burn out," Myra concurs, at the same time enjoying the glee of a child watching fireworks for the first time. Standing at the end of the walk between the house and the curb, she wears neither a coat nor a sweater, and the late-autumn night temperature has dropped to just above freezing.

"Come on, Ma." Elliott puts his arm around his mother-in-law and leads her back into the house.

*** *

All the time Marco was dying, he and Joanna never spoke of the inevitable. "Sit down. Stay," he would say whenever she got up to leave, and she wished she had stayed so many times before when he was healthier and robust and he had asked the same of her. But she had run off to do some errand of little consequence, creating emotional distance between them, readying herself for that inevitable. Marco had made his own preparations by making Joanna privy to his financial holdings, reassuring her that all was in order for

Myra's support and the incidentals: the funeral, the meal afterward, the headstone, the church—dreaded instructions Joanna had entertained with resistance. Now she prepared herself by going alone to the funeral home to make arrangements. It was one of the most difficult tasks she had ever faced. The most difficult had been arranging her daughter, Jill's, funeral. Because Jill's death had been the result of a tragic accident, Joanna had floated through the days, anesthetized with tranquilizers that made the whole incident surreal; only later did reality come crashing down around her. This was different. The process was methodical, and tasks were dealt with as they would have been for a birthday party or a family reunion. These assignments she completed however with reluctance, as though every step was hindered by a wad of chewing gum that made it difficult to put one foot in front of the other. Something weighed her down, held her back, and stifled her speech—a sadness she had never wanted to feel again.

Maybe that was why she had returned over and over again to the mystery of the promise. Whenever her mind was freed of hospice instructions, when the visitors were gone and the coffee cups washed and put away, the plates of cake sealed in plastic wrap and the counter washed down, the promise gnawed at her.

"Mom, did you and Dad keep secrets from me?" She decided to ask her mother straight out as she prepared her for bed in Joanna's childhood room. But there was no longer any direct line to her mother's mind.

"Who's keeping secrets?" Myra responded.

"That's what I'm asking."

"All parents keep secrets."

"Are there any you'd like to tell me now? Any you think I should know?"

"Yes."

"What?"

"You snore. Last night when you slept here with me, you were snoring. You've always snored."

"Mom, I don't snore, and I didn't sleep with you last night. You slept alone."

"You know, you're a bitch, Jenny," her mother said. Jenny had been a high school friend who had stolen Myra's first boyfriend and whom Myra had never forgiven. "And where's my daughter? She hasn't come home."

"I'm right here, Mom."

"You're confused. My daughter is a little girl. I didn't give birth to you."

On another day, when Joanna was paying her parents' bills, she found herself rummaging through the cubbies and drawers of their Chippendale writing desk. Surely, there would be a letter of some kind, an engraved piece of jewelry, something to indicate the woman or man her parents had been sworn to secrecy about and the child that must have been involved—a brother or sister somewhere who would be remembered in her father's will. She already knew about her father's fascination with the man in Italy: in that unprecedented exchange between father and daughter, Marco had emptied his heart on the ride home from the oncologist on the day he was handed his death sentence, and had done so with the urgency of someone who had swallowed poison. It even crossed Joanna's mind that she had been adopted, that her parents had lied to her all these years, and now her mother was begging her father to take the secret to his grave. But she couldn't have been adopted. After all, Myra and Marco's names were on her birth certificate; besides, she looked just like her father.

When she thought her father was dozing, she went into his cufflink drawer. Finding nothing, she rifled her mother's jewelry box, the repository of every piece of evidence in mystery novels. Again, nothing except gaudy pins, strings of dingy fake pearls and clip-on, earrings that her mother hadn't put on in decades. The good stuff was in the safety deposit box at the bank. She turned to her mother's dresser where, along with panties, girdles, and bras, she found a rotting banana, two oranges, and an apple. Lately her mother kept toothpaste and cosmetics in the refrigerator; she combed her hair with a fork.

"What are you looking for, nosey?" her father murmured, eyes closed. He was having a good day, as opposed to those he slept away.

"Just admiring Mom's jewelry."

"Trinkets," he said. "Garbage."

"I guess so."

"I don't know why women want them. Joanna—"

"What is it, Dad?" she asked eagerly.

"I'm thirsty."

Later that night, while they lay exhausted in their own bed at home, Joanna turned to her husband. "Elliott, if you had an affair, would you keep it from me?"

"Depends."

That was not the answer she had been expecting. "What do you mean?"

"Some things, once they're over with, are more menacing than when they were alive. Didn't you ever hear the expression: Let dying dogs lie?"

"But you might tell me and make me promise not to tell anyone. And if Jill were still with us, you would certainly not want her to know."

"Perhaps."

"But you didn't have an affair, did you?"

"No."

"Are you telling me the truth?"

"Joanna, there's another expression you have trouble remembering: Don't beat a dead horse." He winced. "I'm sorry," he quickly offered. He waited for a lecture on insensitivity, or for Joanna to turn completely sullen on him. After all, injuries resulting from a fall from a horse had caused their daughter's death.

"It's all right, Elliott," she reassured him.

Heartened that they seemed to have turned a corner in their relationship, he closed his eyes and breathed easily.

"Elliott, do I snore?"

"Yes. Sometimes," he mumbled before drifting off.

***

Marco wore a ski cap to preserve his body heat. Bald from chemotherapy, he reflected that Ficola men never lost their hair but carried a lush white carpet of it to the grave.

"Well, you like to be different," Joanna told her father as she lay on top of the covers alongside him. She stroked his hand, aware of its warmth and the pulse beating beneath the wafer-like skin spotted from too much sun and IV needles. She sought to emblaze in her mind the sensations of life that inhabited his body but that would soon leave him cold. On bad days she spent the night with him in order to be there when he needed to use the bedpan or take a sip of water or be helped onto his side. She cradled him in her arms and sang to him the way he had to her when she was a little girl burning up with scarlet fever or enduring the pain of mumps or the itchiness of measles. They reminisced about the time he had gotten out of bed and come downstairs in his bare feet—he was never without shoes except when he slept—to chew out a boyfriend of hers who had brought her home too late—despite the fact that Joanna had been 22 at the time and a college graduate working her first job. She made her father laugh. She did all the things for him she wished she had been there to do for Jill when she died. She was not going to miss her father's last breath and the chance to comfort him on his passage from this life to the next.

"Nah," her father whispered with some effort.

He was right; he didn't like to be different. He was a straight shooter.

"Is that my watch you're wearing, Joanna?" he asked about the dime store bargain he found years ago that was still ticking.

"Yeah."

"It's too big on you, *cara*."

"I like wearing it."

He smiled.

"Where's your mother?" he asked.

"She's sleeping, Dad."

"In your old room?" It was important that he knew where she was sleeping now that his illness had forced them to spend their nights apart.

"Yes. In my room."

"Take care of her."

"I will. Don't worry."

"Promise?"

"I promise, Dad."

But that was a promise her father asked *her* to make. What had been the promise her mother had asked her father to make? What could he possibly do for her now, or when he was dead?

"Did Mom ask you to make me promise to look after her?" she asked.

"You kidding? She doesn't think she needs looking after. That's the problem, Joanna. Your mother never asks for anything."

Then what did she ask you for the last night you climbed the stairs? she wanted to say. But asking this would have been wrong; it would have been as if she'd asked to watch her parents making love. Either he would have to volunteer the information or she would have to find out on her own.

***

"I want Frank Sinatra played at the Mass," Myra told Joanna on one of the days she had gone out to make the arrangements while the sweet hospice aide cared for her father.

"Mom, I told you, the priest said no. Only one other speaker besides himself, and no secular music."

"Then go somewhere else."

She had. She'd talked to the pastor at Good Shepherd and also at Saint Agatha's. Both had given her the same answer.

"It's a monopoly, Mom."

"Then go to a different kind of church. Go to a synagogue."

"He's not Jewish."

"But I am."

"You converted 54 years ago."

The news stunned her. "I still want Frank Sinatra," she said.

How was Joanna to deal with a dying father and a mother whose brain was also dying but whose body was alive enough to drive Joanna mad with unreasonable demands? After one of his better days, she approached her father and brought up the funeral.

"Dad, do you have any requests for—you know?"

"The funeral?" He said what she couldn't.

"Yes."

"No. I told you a long time ago I don't believe in any of it anymore."

"Not even reincarnation that we talked about?"

"I know you think Jill's come back in the body of that child you met in Italy. I say seeing is believing, or in this case dying is believing."

"She wants Frank Sinatra."

"Who?"

"Mom. She wants Frank Sinatra singing at your service, but the priests say no."

"Then find a way. Give her what she wants. That's what I care about. That's what matters to me." Then he added: "I think I'd like to be cremated. Yes. I want to be cremated."

And so Joanna went to the Unitarian Society and back to the funeral home and made the tentative arrangements.

***

Joanna's cousins Rosemary and Angie arrive together at Marco's house on the day of his death. Both have come from western Massachusetts, Angie with her husband, Roy, and their 15-month-old son, Michael, and Rosemary with her young gay housemate, Avery. They'll stay with their respective parents in the Medford homes of Raymond and Sal Ficola. Barbara's family will be divided between Joanna's and Nancy's houses. The brother who never left Italy will not be leaving now for his brother's funeral. Could they send him a video of the service? he asked, weeping into the telephone.

As they all sit around the large dining room table, eating the lasagne and salad brought over by Marco and Myra Ficola's neighbor on one side, supplemented by pastries and cookies from the neighbor on their other side, Joanna interrupts the conversation to ask if anyone would like to speak at the service or have Joanna say something for them. "Or maybe there's something you'd like to tell me in private, even if you don't want me to repeat it publicly. Anything at all you'd like me to know about my father."

Silence reigns. Mystified at first by her rambling, they soon disregard the statement, chalking it up to Joanna's grief and exhaustion, and the sounds of forks scraping dishes, crusty bread being broken, soda bottles being opened, and chewing resumes. She will get no secrets from this crowd, or so she thinks.

"Joanna has something to show you all," Elliott announces.

"I do?"

"Yes. The portrait."

"Oh, I don't know, Elliott. It's not quite finished."

"It's terrific. I'll get it."

She has finished it. While she never returned to the images of the Virgin after the incident at St. Mary's hospital, she found that from that day on, she saw everything more deeply, perceived every moment more clearly. When her father was diagnosed with cancer, she had felt compelled to paint him, no longer terrified to depict the human condition.

"It's very nice," Myra says politely when Elliott returns with the unframed canvas and places it on the buffet for all to see. "Who is it?"

"It's wonderful!" Jean-Georges says, throwing up his hands and dropping them back down with gusto onto the table. His right hand lands on Angie's, who's sitting beside him. "Pardon," he says, removing his hand and calling attention to a crimson Angie.

"God, Jean, you probably broke her hand," Nancy says.

"Did I hurt you?" A contrite Jean-Georges (his charming accent deepening his regret) takes Angie's hand in his and gently examines the fingers. "Maybe Elliott should have a look."

Before Elliott can take a step toward Angie, she jumps up, claiming she needs to check on her napping son, and runs out of the room.

"But I am so sorry," Jean-Georges says to Nancy, convinced now that he has really injured Angie.

"I think she's fine," Elliott says, exchanging a knowing glance with Nancy.

"He looks frightened," Barbara says, shifting attention back to the painting. "But then, that's understandable, given his illness."

"I don't think he looks frightened at all," Avery says. "I think he looks like he has a secret."

"You should talk," Norma mutters.

"What did you say, Aunt Norma?" Rosemary asks.

"Stay quiet," Joe says to his wife. "Always have to put in your two cents."

"No, Norma is right," Rosemary's mother, Frances, says. A timid woman, she's the oldest of the sisters-in-law and generally avoids conflict.

"Well, it's about time," Nancy's mother, Vita, says, congratulating her sister-in-law on expressing an opinion on her daughter's situation.

"*Mannaggia!*" Joe curses what his wife's indiscretion has led to.

"No, no." Avery waves his hand in the air. "I deserved it. It isn't fair to leave you all in the dark. But I want you to know that I have told Rosemary why I went to prison. I killed someone." He stares at Rosemary, sending a chill across the table. "Not intentionally, of course. Out of negligence. But it was murder all the same. I had too much to drink one night. I had an accident—a head-on—and the woman in the other car died." He takes a moment, then whispers: "She had two young children."

"How awful," Joanna says. "For all of you."

"I also want to say that I appreciate the kindness this family has shown me. I've never had a large family—or a close one, for that matter. I'll be moving out of Rosemary's place."

"It's not because of what he did," Rosemary says. "I've known about it for quite some time. I'd just like to live alone now. Avery and I will still be good friends, of course."

They shift in their seats. When Angie returns to the table, she's greeted by a new sobriety. As she takes her place between Nancy and Jean-Georges, she avoids looking at either of them. Nancy reaches over to Angie's lap and pats her hand the way she used to when they were in grade school and Angie was the object of some cruel boy's ridicule. That Angie finds Nancy's husband attractive does not concern or surprise Nancy. What troubles her is that her cousin torments herself over it. Angie's vulnerability has always set her apart from others.

"What did my brother have to say about his portrait?" Joe asks Joanna, shifting everyone's focus back to the painting.

"Gregory Peck I'm no longer."

They chuckle softly, as though they can't allow themselves a hearty laugh. Joanna doesn't tell them that after saying this, her father cried because—she knew—she had captured the complexity of his soul.

***

Just as she wanted, Myra wears her blue two-piece outfit to the wake and the funeral, and Joanna thinks her mother looks lovely on the crisp, colorful fall morning. The blue brings out Myra's eye color, still clear and sparkling for her age. What does black have to do with death? Joanna wonders. Her cousin Rosemary is wearing lime green, Barbara red. Joanna finds their choices uplifting. She gets in her car and dashes back to Cambridge to change into a white knit sheath. Basic black might be classy at weddings and cocktail hours, but it's not something to wear when celebrating her father's life, she decides.

Only she and the Unitarian minister speak at the service; it's not her family's custom to eulogize in public. And there have been no revelations about her father. Jill would have spoken about her grandfather, Joanna thinks. It is Elliott, however, who surprises Joanna. Elliott—husband, man of science—looking somewhat awkward but determined, reads a poem he wrote the night before about his beloved father-in-law. Frank Sinatra sings: "I'll be seeing you ..."

Where have you gone, Papà? Joanna says to herself as she and Elliott drive her mother to the restaurant where the mourners will down a five-course meal. Suddenly the trunk of the car pops open.

"That's odd." Elliott pulls over to the curb to shut it.

Why don't you ever clean all this crap out of your trunk, Elliott? Joanna hears her father say. She caresses the watch on her wrist; the touch on her skin is her father's.

At the restaurant they sit at one long table. From his high chair, Angie's toddler, Michael, stares at the ceiling in a corner of the room. Laughing, he points.

"What is it, Mikey?" Angie asks.

"Uncle Marco!" he screams with delight.

"Uncle Marco isn't here, sweetheart." Angie glances over at her aunt, hoping the outburst hasn't upset her.

But Myra sits content and unruffled. "They always come to the little ones," she says, smiling. And Joanna wonders if this could have been the promise: to give her mother a sign, to tell her whether there is life after death. She likes to think this is so. She can believe this is so, because her father, who adamantly refused to entertain matters related to the hereafter, would have done this and much more for her mother. That, Joanna, she hears him clear as a bell, is the miracle—the miracle of unconditional love.

He's here with them. But for how long? Does he want to tell them he's happy? No. She doesn't believe for a minute that he's happy to be away from his family. And for a moment she too sees him—young and healthy, floating high in the corner, smiling with resignation; his only suffering now is to be separated from them in a world that skeptical Marco has had to see for himself.

Then he's gone.

Joanna will look for him, convinced that she'll find him one day, on a train or a plane, standing beside her in a hospital parking lot, in a café in the mountains of Italy, in a child running down the green hills. She'll see him; she'll hear his voice—male or female—and she'll know that it's her father.

Acknowledgements

Throughout the writing of this book my parents were healthy and of sound mind. However, this is very much a book about the supernatural, as well as love, and loss, and I feel compelled to say that, while I was writing about a beloved home going up in flames, a neighbor's house burned down. By the time this printed edition of the collection emerged, my father had developed cancer, albeit a different form than Marco's, and died, and my mother was indeed suffering from dementia.

I am deeply thankful to my steadfast agent, Laura Gross, who first published a slightly altered version of this collection as an eBook, and to her patient former assistant Amaryah Orenstein. To Michael Mirolla and everyone at Guernica Editions who cared enough to bring it to life on the printed page. To Joann Kobin, Betsy Hartmann, Mordicai Gerstein, Roger King, Anthony Giardina, and Carina Wohl for listening and reading. Barbara Silvestri, Darcy Guimond, Emily Friedan, Barry Feingold, and Marci Yoss, gracious contributors of time and facts. My editor and miracle worker, Chris Jerome. My parents, Viola and Michael Labozzetta, who taught me everything I've ever really needed to know in life; Papa, you are forever with me in so many facets of this world, as well as in my heart and mind. My grandfather, Antonino Labozzetta, for his wisdom, and my uncle, Gino Medori, for stumbling upon a singular villa. To my numerous cousins, without whom my childhood would have been very lonely. My children, Ariana, Carina, Michael, and Mark, who keep me in the 21st century. My grandchildren, Ethan and Luke, who give me joy and hope. And, as always, my wonderful husband Martin, who makes all things possible.

Several of these stories have previously appeared in a somewhat different form in literary magazines and journals: "The Swap" and "Pretty Face" in *Perigee*; "Comfort Me, Stranger" in *American Fiction*; and "Forecast for a Sunny Day" in *Italian Americana*.

About the Author

Marisa Labozzetta is the author of the award-winning novel *Sometimes it Snows in America,* and *Stay With Me, Lella.* Her collection of stories, *At the Copa,* was a finalist for the 1999 Binghamton University John Gardner Fiction Award and received a Pushcart nomination. *Thieves Never Steal in the Rain* was an Eric Hoffer eBook award winner. Her work has appeared in *The American Voice, Beliefnet.com, The Florida Review, The Penguin Book of Italian American Writing, Show Me a Hero: Great Contemporary Stories About Sports, When I Am an Old Woman I Shall Wear Purple,* among other publications. She lives in Northampton, Massachusetts.

A reading group guide to *Thieves Never Steal in the Rain* is available at www.marisalabozzetta.com.

Printed in - XLOQ
by 5 DSL GR ,/ L Y U H V
0 RQ WQp Deo